Born in 1962, Valery Ronshin graduated with a degree in history from Petrozavodsk University in Karelia and went on to study at the Literature Institute in Moscow. He now lives in St Petersburg. He started writing relatively late but broke into top literary magazines almost immediately. Ronshin says that for the first thirty years he was "just living a life", moving from one provincial town to another and traveling on foot in Central Russia. He worked at different menial jobs and taught history for a spell before becoming a professional writer. As such, his greatest debt is to Daniil Kharms, the acknowledged Russian master of the absurd. Like Kharms, Ronshin is also a successful children's author with more than 20 books to his name. Unlike Kharms, he wrote the first detective novel for Russian young adults. Ronshin, whose children's stories appeal to grown-ups as well, considers that "a writer's job is to describe his age and die."

valery ronshin

Living a Life

Totally Absurd Tales

glas

GLAS NEW RUSSIAN WRITING

contemporary Russian literature in English translation

Volume 29

The Editors of the Glas series
Natasha Perova & Arch Tait & Joanne Turnbull

On the front cover: detail from a poster by an unknown artist of the 1920s
Camera-ready copy: Tatiana Shaposhnikova

GLAS Publishers
tel./tax: +7(095)441 9157
e-mail: perova@glas.msk.su
www.russianpress.com/glas
www.russianwriting.com

**As of 2002, Glas is distributed in North America by
NORTHWESTERN UNIVERSITY PRESS.**
Chicago Distribution Center, 11030 South Langley Avenue
Chicago, IL 60628, USA
tel: 1-800-621-2736 or 773-568-1550
fax: 1-800-621-8476 or 773-660-2235

ISBN 5-7172-0060-9

Printed at the 'Nauka' printing press, Moscow

CONTENTS

Laughing at Death:
The Prose of Valery Ronshin

by José Alaniz

Towards the end of Valery Ronshin's "Living a Life," the glum hero Trostnikov makes a startling discovery: a freak accident has killed all the other characters in the story. Similarly, at the end of "Taman" an itinerant writer named Ronshin bemusedly stumbles on a critical secret shared by the people with whom he's just been dining: they're — uh, oh — all dead.

These recurring scenes, in which characters discover themselves or others to be dead, yet still very much "alive," beg the question: what constitutes death for the author? In a Ronshin work, you indeed might never even realize you are dead, and even if you do, it hardly seems to matter. The borderline between the living and, shall we say, the "living-challenged" blurs into irrelevance for Ronshin; again and again he draws attention to that imaginary line merely to dismiss it. What's more, the infectious humor of his tales makes death very much a laughing matter.

Disarmingly simple, reliant on archetypes such as the intellectual, the sexy ingenue and the mysterious foreigner, Ronshin's stories evoke the stark realia of Russian urban life, while superimposing a comedic and unpredictable fantasy world. This, of course, was the technique of Daniil Kharms, the absurdist founder of the dada-like OBERIU (Society of Real Art) in 1920s St. Petersburg, whose violent and death-filled nonsense tales take place against the background of ordinary streets and apartments. Kharms, a repressed writer killed by the Soviets in 1941, has enjoyed a (posthumous) renaissance in the late/post-Soviet period, partly because, as numerous critics have pointed out, he was in a sense a realist; he was describing through an exaggerated and distorted lens the atrocities of his time - the violent and purge-filled 1930s.

The demolition of a person, through the Cheshire-cat-like naming and negation of various features and limbs, prefigures Ronshin's erasure of the body in much of his own prose. Both writers engage in a curious de-somatization: they tend to visit death and destruction on oddly mannequin-like or ethereal bodies.

Ronshin's characters do not bleed or break bones; they often don't really die at all. His figures operate in a recognizably Soviet late-stagnation and early-perestroika era, yet his minimalist settings remain curiously timeless. As in Kharms' works, hours, days, years, are measured in the psychological movements of characters' subjectivity: swoons, boredom, endlessly repeated drudgery, blinks, reverie or moment-by-moment awareness. Death as absence, as annihilation, never quite fully enters such a picture.

All the same, Ronshin constantly invokes mortality — albeit a rather lively version of it. Exhumed coffins often turn up empty, or contain the wrong body (which is not really dead anyway); reincarnation figures as commonplace; death, in its time-honored guise of a beautiful woman, smiles for a photograph. Even in a story such as "Eternal Return," in which the two main characters really do "die" at the end, the story's title — to say nothing of its humorously drawn theme of reincarnation — makes nonsense of the notion that they have disappeared, never to come back. On the contrary: "coming back" is their eternal Nietzschean curse.

Having broken through the threshold into Ronshin's afterlife, these characters often find themselves trapped, their freedom curtailed, beset by forces they cannot control, making Ronshin's work as indebted to Kafka as to Kharms. The mood, more often than not one of parody, bemused jest and light black humor, nonetheless carries a tension, an air of imminent threat. Hamsters on a mill going nowhere fast, these figures chaotically stumble from episode to episode, set piece to set piece, in a downward spiral of absurdity. Some, with Ronshin, would consider this a fair description of contemporary Russian daily life — one of both stultifying repetition and dangerous unpredictability.

Another contributor to the sense of a timeless, inescapable recurrence in these works is the author's repeated use of the same stock figures and names, which regularly appear in the stories playing different "roles": Makarov, usually a vain writer on the make; Ronshin, the author's introjection into his narratives; Schulz, a mysterious Woland-like figure who usually plays the part of mad scientist; an evil dwarf; cats; the standard vulgarian alcoholic; the virginal yet seductive Poe-like heroine, who oddly enough often appears as a whore. Clearly, these characters and types are taken as much from Dostoyevsky, science fiction and other sources as from Ronshin's own imaginings, and much of the humor in the stories derives from unpacking these intertextual games.

This revolving repertory cast, whose members reliably die, come back, suffer torments and reappear freshly reconstituted in each succeeding story, recalls Sigmund Freud's observation: "In the realm of fiction we find the plurality of lives which we need. We die with the hero with whom we have identified ourselves; yet we survive him, and are ready to die again just as safely with another hero."

And so we ask the question once more: what does death "mean" for Ronshin? And how does Ronshin's realist credo, "A writer should describe his age and die," serve to inform us about post-Soviet Russian culture?

That, reader, will be left to you to discover. But whether as absurdist, "realist" or just a plain good yarn-spinner, Valery Ronshin — the Daniil Kharms of his era — reassures us of one thing: it's okay to laugh at death. If you dare.

> from *Necrotopia: Discourses of Death & Dying in Late/Post-Soviet Russian Culture* by José Alaniz

Living a Life

Living a Life

Translated by Joanne Turnbull

Trostnikov lived on the fourth floor of an old three-story building. To get to his room, you had to go past the first floor, home to the girl Inna, who for years now had been waiting for True Love; go up to the second floor, home to Professor Elenevsky and his young wife Muse (an art critic by profession, a train station floozy by calling); then go up to the third floor, home to the snitch Parfyonov, who snitched on everyone he could; turn to the right, climb a narrow iron staircase; turn to the left and run into a filthy door.

Behind this door, in a room always a shambles, on a bed always a shambles, lolled the always sleepy Trostnikov.

He was a philosopher. Because he had various philosophical thoughts. Mostly other people's. Trostnikov wrote them down in a notebook.

The first thought in the notebook was this: *Life is a dream.*

And so he slept. Seventy-two hours at home. Twenty-four hours at work.

Trostnikov worked as a watchman at some bogus outfit where he had his own trestle bed. Over this bed hung a board with a list of the employees. Turnover was high. People came and went all the time. Trostnikov noted neatly in pencil: *fired... on vacation... out sick... dead...* Old Manya had lasted longer than anyone else at this outfit. She had arrived as a 17-year-old girl and now she was past seventy.

Old Manya was a philosopher, too. No matter what she talked about, she always talked about death. She would begin in a roundabout way:

"Sometimes, at the front, I'd be dragging a wounded man —

bullets whistling by: fyut! fyut! fyut! — and I'd just keep right on. Never did stop to think I could've been killed..."

"Why are you telling me all this?" Trostnikov would wonder from his trestle bed.

"No reason," Old Manya replied philosophically. "I'll be dead soon. Then you'll remember that once there was that old Manya."

Besides Old Manya, the outfit employed the drunk Grisha and the former military pilot Rusanov, also a drunk. They mostly drank leg lotion.

Opposite the outfit, across a small dirty river, stood a children's toy factory. Every night, military conveyances came for the toys...

It was near the end of the day. Time stood still. The clock on the Central Post Office had said five past two for the last ten years. Professor Elenevsky was on television. Looking intelligent and talking nonsense.

Trostnikov ambled down the street. When he didn't have other people's thoughts in his head, he was compelled to think his own.

Is today Monday or Wednesday? he racked his brain.

At an intersection, Trostnikov noticed the girl Inna. She was staring into a puddle on the asphalt.

"Look," said the girl Inna, "you can see the clouds in the sky."

Trostnikov looked but, aside from a soggy cigarette end, didn't see anything.

"Is today Monday or Wednesday?" he asked the girl Inna.

"Today is Sunday," she said. "And yesterday, coming out of the entrance, you bumped right into me and didn't even notice."

Trostnikov looked at Inna, not understanding what she was saying.

Um-hmm, he thought dully. *If you can't think straight, there's nothing I can do.*

It started to drizzle.

"I love the rain!" the girl Inna skipped with delight. "I don't like umbrellas."

Arms spread wide, she began spinning round and round.

Is she drunk or what? Trostnikov was at a loss.

"All the world's flaws are in me," said the girl Inna. "That's why sometimes I feel a little sad at heart..."

Trostnikov decided to flaunt his intelligence.

"Everything in life is relative," he said pompously. "For example, compared to some sad sack freezing in Siberia, you're very well off. But if we compare you to a princess, then she probably has it better..."

The girl Inna looked distressed.

"You say I'm not a princess and that hurts me a little. Every woman wants to be a princess."

"There are too many people in the world," sighed Trostnikov. "You can't be a princess for all of them."

"But what about for one of them? My one and only..."

"Well, maybe," Trostnikov winced.

This idiotic conversation was making him tired. He just wanted to get to work and lie down.

He quickened his step. The girl Inna kept pace.

"You've lived in our building for three years," she said. "And yet we don't know anything about each other. Even that unpleasant old man Parfyonov always asks me what I'm reading, where I'm going, who I'm seeing... But you never ask me anything, never care..."

"Doesn't matter, doesn't matter," Trostnikov waved the girl Inna away like an annoying fly.

He practically ran.

"It does to a woman — a lot," said the girl Inna, barely able to keep up. "If you'd just say, 'Hello, Inna,' when we meet, it would make me feel good."

Trostnikov jumped onto a trolleybus and was gone.

"Oof," he wiped his damp forehead. "What a pain in the ass. She is such an idiot."

The smokestacks were smoking at the children's toy factory. Time continued to stand still. The boss Ivlev looked in on the supine Trostnikov, poked him in the knee, and read him the riot act:

"You're a watchman! It's your duty — your duty! — to go on rounds, answer the phone, and sweep the floor!"

"Fuck off!" Trostnikov replied, without opening his eyes.

He knew how to talk to simple people.

The boss Ivlev backed straight down, sat on the edge of the trestle bed, and began a story:

"Yesterday, swear to God, I went fishing..."

Trostnikov didn't hear him. He was already asleep. And when he woke up, he was home.

"He says the damnedest things!" Trostnikov sighed.

"That's nothing," said the former pilot Rusanov. "Once I fell asleep on the tram and woke up in the drunk tank."

The snitch Parfyonov was drinking tea at the local greasy spoon. He would take a swallow, take the candy out of his mouth, put it on the wrapper, spoon some brown pulp out of a jar and into his mouth, quickly chew it up, put the candy back in his mouth, take a swallow of tea, take the candy out of his mouth, eat a spoonful of pulp... And so on.

"How are you?" Parfyonov fixed his keen eyes on Trostnikov.

"Fine," replied Trostnikov.

The snitch Parfyonov dug around in the jar with his spoon.

"Why the kindergarten answer? 'Fine.' You must be more specific."

"More specifically: I eat, I sleep, I talk."

"Well, now, that's better," the snitch Parfyonov slurped his tea. "Now we have a topic for an interro... for a conversation. Eat when? Sleep with whom? Talk about what?"

"What's it to you?" Trostnikov didn't understand. "What are you, undercover?"

He suspects, the creep, Parfyonov thought, furiously sucking his candy.

It was drizzling. His body ached. His mind was a muddle. Trostnikov looked out the window. Outside it was the same as yesterday.

Trostnikov sat down at the table and opened his notebook.

What should I write? he nibbled his pen drearily.

He didn't have any thoughts. Other people's or his own.

Trostnikov went downstairs. On the first floor, the girl Inna was still waiting for True Love.

"Want me to tell you my innermost thoughts?" she asked Trostnikov.

Trostnikov walked right past her. By the entrance, Professor Elenevsky's young wife Muse was smoking a casual cigarette. A big black car rolled up. And rolled away with Muse.

Professor Elenevsky continued to look intelligent and talk nonsense on television...

The drunk Grisha was, as usual, pie-eyed, but wearing a white shirt.

"Got married," he boasted.

"Where'd you dig her up?" Old Manya scoffed.

"They'll give us an apartment soon," the drunk Grisha was bursting with self-satisfaction. "She's the worst kind of invalid."

"Why'd you marry a cripple?" Trostnikov didn't understand.

The drunk Grisha gave him a sly wink.

"Just the person to marry. I can relax — she won't tempt anyone."

Old Manya was discoursing on death:

"Being burned's no fun. But being drownded, you don't want that either. Cemeteries are in low places. Mighty boggy come fall. In the *conservatorium*, though, they say the temperature's enough to raise the dead..."

"*Crematorium*," the drunk Grisha corrected her. "You bumpkin."

"Wish I'd drop dead," Old Manya droned on. "Living's become a nightmare. People are worse than dogs... But God won't let me die. And I can't very well be buried alive..."

It was a humid night. Trostnikov lay drenched in sweat. He couldn't fall asleep.

"He-e-e-lp!" a woman's voice exploded outside his window.

The night is full of evil, Trostnikov wrote in his notebook.

It was early March. Everything was melting away. Including Trostnikov's money. In the women's changing room they were singing something Russian and long-drawn-out...

"Those broads've been guzzling again," the former pilot Rusanov remarked. "They get pickled every day, the bitches."

Trostnikov was eating a bologna sandwich. The drunk Grisha looked on with hungry eyes. He had spent his last ruble on beer three days ago.

"Ah, the songs we sang when I was young," Grisha sighed nostalgically, swallowing saliva. "You never heard the likes o' them. *A bit of skirt was hightailing it up Broadway.* Or this one! *Hey, boy, don't you drink from that john! The germs'll send you to the back of beyond!*"

As Trostnikov was finishing his sandwich, a piece of bologna fell on the dirty floor. The drunk Grisha swooped down and stuffed it fussily in his mouth.

"You wouldn't have eaten it off the floor anyway," he explained to Trostnikov.

Whatever you give away is yours, Trostnikov pulled out his notebook and wrote.

Thursday dawned. Or maybe Friday. Trostnikov ambled down the street, reading all the signs in turn. A warm summer rain started, then stopped. A rainbow hung in the sky. The girl Inna was skipping along, clutching her sandals in one hand.

"I love to run through puddles barefoot," she laughed. "It makes me feel as though I'm not really me. It's so wonderful..."

Trostnikov looked at her bright face and thought, *Soon I'll grow old and die.* As if to illustrate his thought, a black van went by with the sign *On his final journey.*

At home Trostnikov wrote in his notebook: *I do not exist. Even though I'm sitting in an armchair under a lampshade.* He put his pen down and thought. The last sentence struck him as rather odd. He owned neither an armchair, nor a lampshade. Trostnikov got up and walked over to the mirror. In the mirror he could see the chair, the table, the floor... But not himself.

I've philosophized myself out of existence, Trostnikov took fright and rushed out in search of a psychiatrist.

"Follow me," a nurse in a short lab coat beckoned him down the hall.

Trostnikov stared at her long legs. And his imagination ran away with him... away with him...

Stop that, right now! Trostnikov reproached himself. *You're a philosopher, after all!*

They were outside the psychiatrist's office.

"Vadim Nikolaevich, there's another nutcase here to see you," said the nurse, opening the door a crack.

"Well, let me see him!" came the merry reply.

"You may go in," said the nurse.

Trostnikov found the psychiatrist seated at his desk.

"So, you're nuts are you?" he inquired cheerfully, rubbing his hands together. "Happens all the time. Can you imagine what would happen if the whole world went nuts?"

"Sure I can," Trostnikov nodded.

"Well, then, what's the problem?" He gave Trostnikov a wink. "You think you're a vampire-horse?"

"I feel like I don't exist," said Trostnikov.

"Since when have you felt like this?"

"Since Friday."

The psychiatrist thought for a long time. Then he asked:

"And what's today?"

"Thursday," said Trostnikov.

The psychiatrist thought again for a long time.

"So what does that make?" he said finally. "A week you haven't existed?"

"I guess so."

The psychiatrist was about to have another long think, but Trostnikov got to him first.

"Well?" he asked.

The psychiatrist banged his fist nervously on the desk.

"What's your hurry? What are you, late for a train? Hold your horses!"

"I'm sorry," Trostnikov mumbled.

"Ever had the mumps?"

"No."

"Syphilis?"

"No."

The psychiatrist wrote all this down. Then he said:

"You may go. You're perfectly healthy."

"What do you mean healthy?" Trostnikov protested. "I don't exist!"

The psychiatrist hemmed.

"So what? Is that any reason to go nuts? For all I know, I don't exist either. One person doesn't have any money... Another one doesn't have any children... *Son cosas de la vida*, as the Spanish say. That's life."

Trostnikov walked out into the street. Soldiers were marching by. Prostitutes were smoking by the hotel. Underground, metro trains were hurtling along. The former pilot Rusanov was telling about the time he went head to head with a Nazi ace!

"Umm, those were the days," Rusanov puffed on a cigarette. "Flew head to head with a Nazi ace! *It's all over*, I thought. *I'm a dead duck!* But I never thought of veering away..."

Trostnikov was asleep. Beyond the window snow was falling. Beyond the snow Parfyonov was slinking. The barbed wire on top of the wall around the children's toy factory was electrified. Then someone else's thoughts surfaced. Trostnikov, without waking, wrote them down... Downstairs the girl Inna sat by the window, waiting for True Love.

"I don't need anything," she never tired of saying. "Only love. My soul yearns for nothing but love."

"That's your problem," Trostnikov replied and went off to have his picture taken for his identification card.

"Come on, give me a smile!" the photographer chided. "This isn't for your gravestone."

Trostnikov examined the finished snapshots. An old, haggard face...

A strong wind blew. Bits of trash flew up from garbage bins and whirled over the city. Crows perched on the bins and cawed.

Cawed...

Trostnikov lay on his trestle bed. Old Manya lumbered up.

"You still laying about," she looked askance.

"What do you mean `laying about'?" Trostnikov said limply. "Can't you see I'm standing up?"

"Weren't any good people before, and there ain't any now," Old Manya went on grumbling under her breath. "Just dregs!"

The boss Ivlev was bored to distraction.

"Maybe I should read something?" he mused aloud. "What do you recommend?"

"Dickens," Trostnikov muttered half asleep.

"Is it about war?"

Dirty clouds sailed across the sky. Two old women had been crushed to death in a meat line. According to a Water Safety Board notice: *Ten people drowned in our region last month, three of them in bathtubs.*

"How sad our lives are," the girl Inna sighed mournfully. "Both close up... and far away..."

Professor Elenevsky went on talking nonsense on television.

"How do these people get to be professors?" Trostnikov wanted to know.

A streetlight swayed in the wind. Dogs barked. Someone banged on a piano.

Fallen leaves rustled underfoot.

A black car rolled up. Professor Elenevsky got out with an air of importance.

"That's all," he let the driver go.

"H'llo," Trostnikov greeted him.

The professor walked right past him.

Old Manya died. Trostnikov noted on his board: *dead.* And talked about her a bit with the former pilot Rusanov:

"At the front, when Old Manya was dragging the wounded

away, and bullets were whistling by — fyut! fyut! fyut! — she just kept right on. Never thought about how she might be killed..."

Rusanov muttered obscenities, as usual.

"She spent the whole war way back in the rear washing foot wrappings. And you actually bought that bunk about 'bullets whistling by — fyut! fyut!' "

Trostnikov turned over onto his other side and fell asleep. Work time went by.

Winter arrived. The country's immortal leader passed away. Trostnikov went to the baths.

"Whadaya want?!" the woman attendant stared at him as though he were mad.

"What do you mean?" Trostnikov didn't understand.

The woman was purple with rage.

"The whole country's in mourning, and you want a bath!"

She went on... and on...

Trostnikov went out into the street. A dirge flowed over the city. Red flags with black ribbons were everywhere. Some guy, his sheepskin coat flapping, was standing in a phone booth bellowing into the receiver:

"But when are we gonna take out the toilet bowl?!"

They buried the country's immortal leader... a year later they buried another... and a year after that a third...

Professor Elenevsky's wife, Muse, was telling a new joke:

"The British Prime Minister says to the American President: 'It's a shame you couldn't come to Moscow for the funeral. The food was splendid!' 'Doesn't matter,' says the President. 'I'll go next year.'"

Everybody laughed. The snitch Parfyonov took notes: *Wif. Prof. Elen. tol. antisov. jo.*

Winter had ended. Now it was summer: humid and buggy. The drunk Grisha's mother came to visit and cried:

"Not long ago, it seems, I was taking him to kindergarten, and now he's been dead these four years."

"What do you mean 'four years'?" Trostnikov raised himself up on one elbow.

Four years!

It seemed like only yesterday that the drunk Grisha had been sitting here and dreaming:

"Ah, wouldn't I like to get sloshed and retch!"

The country was all in an uproar. An excited crowd streamed towards the square. A big bozo with a cross around his neck was unrolling a poster:

"Come One and All! To the Rally in Memory of Masha Sukacheva, Poisoned a Year Ago by the Nectar Cooperative in a Routine Rat Poisoning!

Nectar, Trostnikov sighed. He was in the mood for something sweet. The stores had nothing but cans of pickled sea kale. It was a warm, sunny day. Poplar down wafted about. The girl Inna was sitting on a bench in the yard waiting for True Love. In her hands she held a small volume of verse.

"Say," the girl Inna motioned to Trostnikov with her pointed chin. "Would you like to borrow this book to read?"

"No, I wouldn't," Trostnikov rushed past. "Even without reading it, I know it's junk!"

"Why are you so... implacable?" the girl Inna ran up the stairs after him. "Tell me why?"

"Forgive me," Trostnikov stopped her at the door to his room. "I've just gotten off the night shift. I must rest."

He went to bed. The girl Inna went slowly down the stairs. She was crying one second, laughing the next. Her lips whispered: "I yearn for love and human warmth."

It was Wednesday. Or maybe Tuesday. Trostnikov was doing

two things at once: sleeping and thinking. He thought roughly the same thing as Jesus Christ. Namely: *Lord, why have you forsaken me?*

Summer blazed. The air was stifling. T-shirts stuck repulsively to sweaty bodies. Professor Elenevsky was taken off the air and deprived of his car and driver.

"That's a-a-all right," said the professor with a crooked grin. "We survived the war, we'll survive this. The main thing is to have a good *stool.*"

Now Trostnikov could ask the question that had bothered him for so long.

"Tell me, how do you get to be a professor?"

"Simple," Professor Elenevsky said, openly and honestly, in keeping with the spirit of the times. "Screw the wife of an academician."

Elenevsky's wife, Muse, became chairman of the Animal Rights League. She confined her conversation to the subject of animals.

"Nothing but beasts everywhere!" she constantly insisted.

The snitch Parfyonov admitted to being a snitch. His face stained with tears, he howled hysterically:

"I'm a murderer! A murderer!"

"My God, how can that be?! How can that be?!" The girl Inna cried along with Parfyonov. "Why are we all so unhappy? Why?"

"Good people, I repent," Parfyonov beat his breast. "I was young! They forced me! I informed on my friends!"

Professor Elenevsky clapped him on the shoulder by way of encouragement.

"We're all guilty. We should all repent. Now cheer up, a new life is beginning!"

Summer ended. The "new life" began. Rusanov the former

pilot died. Trostnikov noted on the board: *dead*. And talked about him a bit with the boss Ivlev.

"Once Rusanov flew head to head with a Nazi ace. He thought, *it's all over. I'm a dead duck!* But he never thought of veering away..."

The boss Ivlev muttered obscenities, as usual.

"He spent the whole war on the ground pulling blocks out from under the wheels of planes. And you actually bought that bunk about 'going head to head with a Nazi ace.' "

Yard-keepers scoured sidewalks. Trams rattled by. Snow melted on roofs. Professor Elenevsky became a democrat. He even paid a call on Trostnikov. The professor's wife, Muse, went with him, so did the girl Inna and the former snitch Parfyonov. Trostnikov made them all a coffee drink called *Dawn*.

Muse lit a cigarette and began talking about her new work:

"If a dog bothers you, don't slap its paws, or its head. Give it a good swift kick in the balls."

She took a last puff and tossed the cigarette end into Professor Elenevsky's cup.

"My dear," the offended professor's eyebrows shot up. "I hadn't finished my coffee."

"That goes for men, too," Muse went on talking. "If a man bothers you, a swift kick in the balls is all it takes."

"May I read you a poem?" the girl Inna asked shyly.

Permission was granted.

> *White roses*
> *Wilt in vases,*
> *Patches of moonlight*
> *Speckle the table...*

The former snitch Parfyonov took notes out of habit: *Rea. vers. of dub. cont.*

"Where is your bathroom?" Muse asked loudly. "I want to wash my hands."

"I don't have a bathroom," Trostnikov apologized. "There's water in the kitchen. But only cold."

They went into the kitchen. Muse turned on the faucet. There was no water. *What could I talk to her about?* Trostnikov searched his mind.

"This is your second marriage, isn't it?" he recalled. "Where's your first husband now?"

"Kicked the bucket," Muse devoured him with her eyes. "Why aren't you married? Is it a sexual problem?"

"I'll find a ballerina and marry her."

"Why a ballerina?"

"They don't eat much. More economical."

Muse laughed sensually.

"Would you like to have sex?"

Trostnikov felt hot all over.

"I can't decide," he muttered in embarrassment.

"Well, then, let's decide," Muse pressed up against him with her big breasts.

"Those members of our society who are supposed to be — the intelligentsia — are not very cultivated!" Professor Elenevsky thundered in the next room.

The former snitch Parfyonov scribbled: *Prof. Elen. sland. the int.*

"What is it you're always writing in that little book of yours?" the girl Inna asked good-naturedly. "Poetry?"

The former snitch Parfyonov blushed and tried to jam the notebook in his pocket.

"Um-hm, poetry."

An embarrassed Trostnikov appeared in the doorway followed by an unsatisfied Muse, straightening her skirt.

"Want to hear a new joke?" she burst in. "An intellectual is walking down Nevsky Prospekt and sees a man urinating by the Kazan Cathedral. 'Excuse me,' says the intellectual, 'could you please tell me how to get to the Hermitage?' 'Why go all the way to the Hermitage?' says the man. "You can piss right here.' "

Everyone laughed. The former snitch Parfyonov took notes: *Wif. Prof. Elen. to. ano. anti-Sov. jo.*

Life flowed by, like water. Trostnikov stood on a bridge, watching bits of trash and rotten boards floating on the surface, a dead fish rose belly-up. The air smelled of mold. A little boy ran up.

"Say, mister, have you been here long?"

"Very long," Trostnikov replied.

"Did you see a raft go by?"

"No," said Trostnikov. "I didn't."

The sun was setting. It was time to go to work. To sleep. Trostnikov set off. Coming toward him he saw an angry Muse.

"It's easier to catch the clap than a taxi around here," she snorted. Then added: "Have you heard the news?"

"What news?" Trostnikov frowned.

"Someone snitched on the snitch Parfyonov. He was taken away last night by fighters from the Invisible Front."

"By who?"

"By KGB, that's who."

Trostnikov walked on.

"It wasn't you who snitched on him, was it?" she maliciously called after him.

"Fuck off!" Trostnikov said without turning round.

He knew how to talk to cultivated people.

At work everyone lay dead. The boss Ivlev in his office. The workers in their changing rooms. The women in the women's. The men in the men's.

There had been a radioactive leak at the children's toy factory. Trostnikov noted on the board next to each name: *dead... dead... dead... dead... dead... dead...*

When he got home, Trostnikov went to bed out of habit. But he couldn't sleep. He felt awful, as if someone had bored a screwdriver into his stomach.

Why do I feel so awful? Trostnikov pondered.

The girl Inna came up to see him. She began babbling in her disjointed way:

"The winter is almost over... You must try to live through this winter... don't work, just try to survive..." Her hands fluttered over the supine Trostnikov like two excited butterflies. "You must read good books... naive, kind literature... *The Count of Monte Cristo...* Then the summer will come... it can't not come... It'll be warm... And everything will be all right... all right..."

"But there's something wrong with me," Trostnikov fretted. "Something's really wrong."

The girl Inna's hands again fluttered over Trostnikov's head.

"Just think of Pushkin... of Blok... of Marina Tsvetayeva... Not long ago I discovered... made a small discovery... They didn't die. They're all THERE," the girl Inna pointed to the ceiling where a cracked chandelier was hanging. "They turned into little stars... And they're sort of signalling to us FROM THERE." The girl Inna attempted to show Trostnikov with her fingers how they were signalling.

Trostnikov listened in silence.

"And we won't die," said the girl Inna. "Green grass will grow over our humble graves."

Trostnikov heaved a sigh. He didn't want to be grown over with green grass...

"Something's making me sick."

"I went to Symphony yesterday," the girl Inna didn't hear him. "It was just magical... Debussy... Ravel... People with human faces all around me... Then I took the metro home... Everyone was so dead... so empty..."

"Everything makes me sick," Trostnikov mumbled.

The girl Inna suddenly came out of her reverie. And looked at Trostnikov.

"You have got to go away," she said. "Anywhere."

Trostnikov liked the sound of that: "anywhere." It smacked of something philosophical, even cosmic...

ANY... WHERE...

"I'd like to go away," he said. "I'd like to go to Tahiti. I want to be buried next to Gauguin and Jacques Brel. With the waves lapping nearby."

"Go away..." the girl Inna was off again and rocking evenly back and forth. "Go away... Go away..."

"I'll go!" Trostnikov made up his mind.

He got out of bed and set off for the train station. In the yard a drunken Professor Elenevsky was barking at a stray dog.

"Woof! Woof! Woof!" the professor woofed loudly.

The stray watched him in silence with human eyes.

At the station Trostnikov said to the ticket lady:

"Give me one ticket."

"Where are you going?" asked the lady.

"Wherever's cheapest," Trostnikov replied.

Christlove's Conversations with a 1957 Wireless Set

Translated by Kathleen Cook

"There are noisy people and quiet people, and people who are nothing to write home about," a woman writer once wrote. Not bad. Good enough to steal.

I'll steal it.

Christlove is nothing to write home about.

He's sitting on the floor in his room in a communal apartment, leaning against the warm central heating radiator. And listening, eyes closed, to an old wireless set made in 1957.

The wireless set is talking in a woman's voice:

"Yesterday in Paris..."

"Paris," Christlove whispers. "In Paris..."

"But tomorrow in Singapore..." says the wireless.

"Sing-a-pore," Christlove tries the word out. "Sing-a-pore..."

There is a loud knock on the door. Christlove gives a start.

"Who is it?" he asks in a fright.

"Gestapo. Open up!" comes the reply.

Christlove opens the door.

Raissa, a forty-year-old virgin, is standing on the threshold with a dirty shopping bag in her hand

"Look at this, Christlove," she says. "Some nutcase threw out an almost brand new bag. So I took it — I'm not proud. I can use it to go shopping." Then she adds, as she invariably does: "Get along into the kitchen. I won't be long."

Christlove knows that Raissa will be telling him about some sex film she has seen. She watches sex videos every evening.

Christlove shuffles into the communal kitchen and turns on the light, which sends the cockroaches scuttling in all directions.

Raissa follows and puts the frying pan with slices of fat on the gas stove. There's nothing she likes more than big chunks of crunchy fried fat.

The fat spits noisily while Raissa begins her narration:

"Just a load of rubbish! Take the title: *The Lips Open Girls.* See what they're getting at, Christlove?"

"Oh, yes," Christlove nods, although all he can see are sizzling slices of fat.

Raissa declares firmly as she has done countless times before:

"But I'd never do it, Christlove! Never give myself to a man! Let him stick that thing up me?! No, thank you very much! I'm not that far gone yet. Poor creatures. The things those beasts do to them! I can hardly bear to watch. It's enough to make you fetch up! Today I bought another video called *Strip Down, Girly.* I can just imagine what filth that is..."

Raissa switches her attention to the frying pan. Christlove, liberated, returns to his wireless set.

The wireless set announces in a man's voice this time:

"Yesterday a puma by the name of Juliet escaped from the zoo in Rio de Janeiro..."

"Juliet..." Christlove repeats dreamily.

He has a vision of a beautiful girl with blue eyes, a dark complexion and a sweet oval face. A warm sea breeze is ruffling her chestnut hair and pleated skirt...

But there is nothing under the skirt.

Well, there are legs, of course, but...

Nothing else to speak of.

Juliet races towards Christlove! Christlove races towards Juliet! The waves crash on the sandy shore...

"Ah-ah!" Christlove murmurs ecstatically.

"Juliet has already torn five adults limb from limb..." the newscaster continues impassively.

"Juliet," Christlove sighs. "My Juliet..."

The image of the beautiful girl fades away slowly.

There is a scratching at the door, followed by a hissed whisper: "Christlove!"

"Eh? What's that?" Christlove peers fearfully into the corridor.

"Come here, sonny, come here." Old Ma Utkina's voice reaches him from the depths of the dark corridor.

He sets off along the pitch-black passage.

"Christlove!" A sudden hot-breathed bark by his very ear.

"Ouch!" Christlove gives a frightened yelp.

"Shush!"

Christlove gropes at the wall feverishly, searching for the light switch.

"Don't put the light on," Old Ma Utkina whispers.

"Why not?"

"They might see."

"Who might see?"

"They might." Then, beseechingly, "Go to the baker's, there's a good lad, and get this poor old woman some gingerbread."

"It's too late, Grandma," says Christlove. "The baker's closed."

"And some milk, love." Old Ma Utkina takes no notice. "Gingerbread and milk. Here's a ruble." She clutches Christlove's hand and thrusts the coin into his palm. "Don't forget the change."

Change from a ruble?!

"They just sit there gorging," the old woman moans. "They wait till I go to sleep, then stuff themselves. And let me starve to death."

A bright light goes on suddenly. Seryozha, the old woman's grandson, stands there sneering, by the switch.

"What's up, Bony Legs?"

That's what he calls Old Ma Utkina.

"Nothing, Seryozha, dear, nothing," the old woman mutters nervously and vanishes round the corner in a flash, like a mouse.

Seryozha gives Christlove a newspaper.

"Here, read that. Out loud."

Christlove reads:

"An exhibition of demented artists..."

"Not all of it, stupid, only the bit I've underlined."

Christlove reads the underlined bit.

"...visitors to the exhibition were most impressed by 'The Butcher's Shop', a painting by schizophrenic X. The brightly painted canvas shows a box-room with two butchers carving up the torso of a third. Blood is gushing onto the floor. Through the half-open door we see a shop girl standing by the counter weighing chunks of raw meat for the customers. This unusual fantasy by a schizophrenic could rival Salvador Dali himself..."

"That's me, schizophrenic X. Remember how they put me in the looney bin last year?" Seryozha explains proudly.

Christlove remembers all right. Hadn't Seryozha chased him round the apartment with an axe in his fit of rage?

"A man was done in yesterday in our yard," Seryozha goes on. "There wasn't a word about it on the telly. So not all murders get reported."

"No-o-o," Christlove drawls miserably.

Eventually Seryozha takes pity on Christlove and lets him go.

So here he is again in his little den with his beloved wireless set.

The wireless set is cooing sweetly:

"There is no need to be afraid of death. Death isn't the end but just a door to another life, a better life. So ponder on these words..."

Christlove ponders.

From the corridor comes the sound of the old Communist Zakhar Matveich Zhurbin shuffling from the communal toilet.

He stops at Christlove's door and gives a resolute knock. Christlove opens up.

"Now look here, Christlove," Zakhar Matveich says to him sternly. "You really must clean the toilet properly when it's your turn."

And off he goes to his room, without waiting for a reply, to write his memoirs.

Zhurbin has plenty to remember. As a budding sculptor, he was even commissioned to make the left leg for the statue of Lenin that still adorns the town's central square to this day. He is writing about this particular episode now in his memoirs.

There is a clanging of metal in the wind outside. The rain beats savagely against the windows.

Can it be winter already?

Perhaps everything is covered with snow?

Christlove is afraid to look out of the window. Who can say what might be there?

The wireless set is peeping away — dot dot dot, dash, dash, dash, dot dot dot. Three dots, three dashes and three dots.

Christlove knows that means SOS.

Someone is drowning at sea. Huge waves are crashing over the deck, knocking the helpless victim down and perhaps flinging him overboard.

How awful! How terrible!

But Christlove is nice and safe. With the radiator warming his back. He begins to doze to the accompaniment of the Morse code. And dreams of a puma called Juliet. He is stroking her fur and she is purring:

"Purrr... purrr..."

The purring grows louder, more aggressive. Until suddenly the puma opens her jaws and pounces on Christlove.

Christlove wakes up in a fright, his heart beating furiously, only to find that his life has not changed for the better while he was asleep. He sees the same old room full of rubbish and the same old 1957 wireless set. And in the same old corridor the same old telephone is ringing frantically.

Christlove is afraid of telephone calls... And rings at the door... And cars hooting... And people shouting at him... In fact, he is afraid of everything.

"Christlove!" Raissa bangs on the wall with her fist. "Have you gone deaf, eh? Go and answer the phone!"

Christlove goes into the corridor, picks up the receiver and puts it to his ear.

"Hello."

A stentorian voice nearly splits his eardrum.

"Christlove!"

"Speaking," Christlove responds timidly.

"Commander Gryazev on the line. You will report to your local recruitment centre tomorrow, stupid cunt! Bring a mug, spoon and dry rations for three days. In field dress. Got that, stupid cunt!"

"Alright," says Christlove obligingly.

"'Yessir', not 'alright'!" barks the voice. "Over and out, stupid cunt!"

Beep, beep, beep, come the short pips.

"Yessir!" Christlove yells belatedly.

He puts down the receiver and dashes into the toilet.

Christlove sits on the toilet seat facing three bags hanging on the wall: they contain specially torn strips of newspaper. The Utkin family uses the *Labour* and Raissa subscribes to the *Titbits*, but the old communist Zhurbin prefers the *Truth* and nothing but the *Truth*.

Christlove has no bag of his own. He filches paper surreptitiously from the Utkins, Raissa and Zhurbin in turn.

Today, for example, he takes a few sheets from Raissa's bag and begins to read scraps from "Titbits".

"Dear Editors," says one of them. "I once fell for a boy and had to get an abortion. Then I fell for another boy and had to get another abortion. In the end I grew fed up with boys and began to fall for girls instead. But I don't get any orgasms with them. What should I do? Please help me. Katya Oreshkina, class 5-B."

Another scrap of newspaper has an answer to Katya's letter from a sexologist by the name of Lousey.

"Dear Katya Oreshkina, I know just how you feel! Although I belong to a different generation, my life is a mess too. My wife is a prostitute and my daughter is a drug addict. So, unlike you, I got fed up with girls and began to fall for boys. But I don't get any orgasms from that either..."

The toilet door begins to jig on its battered hinges.

"Christlove!" Raissa yells angrily. "Get a move on! You're not the only one nature calls!"

"Just a moment, Raissa," Christlove cries, straining hard. "I won't be long."

After all these exertions he collapses on the floor, beside his beloved wireless set.

And his beloved wireless set inspires him with new strength. It starts talking in a pleasant female voice:

"Did you know, dear listeners, that most people die in their sleep? About three o'clock in the morning, as a rule. It is now five to three, incidentally. Just imagine how many people have died while

I have been talking. They went to bed yesterday evening and now they will never wake up again."

"Never," Christlove whispers in horror.

"Never," the woman's pleasant voice repeats. "And so, dear listeners, I strongly recommend that you check whether your relatives are really asleep. Or whether they have already embarked on the path to Eternity."

In the absence of any relatives, Christlove goes off to check on his neighbours. First and foremost, of course, Zhurbin, as the most likely candidate for an imminent encounter with Eternity.

"Zakhar Matveich," Christlove knocks quietly on the old communist's door. "Zakhar Matveich..."

There is no reply.

Christlove peeps into the room and sees Zakhar Matveich lying on the bed. But in fact he isn't there at all. All that remains of him are his memoirs.

Christlove leafs through the bulky manuscript.

" 'Now tell me honestly, Comrade Zhurbin?' the First Secretary of the Town Communist Party said to me as one communist to another. 'It's a very responsible job that the Party is entrusting to you. Not everyone has the honour of making a left leg for Lenin. Are you up to it?'

" 'I'll do my very best, Comrade First Secretary,' I replied, gritting my teeth as if I were facing a firing squad."

"Beep, beep, beep," goes the time signal.

Three o'clock.

Christlove hurries back to his room to hear the news. He always listens to the news, although it has absolutely nothing to do with him.

"Floods in China... An earthquake in Greece... Drought in Algeria..."

Without realizing it Christlove falls asleep to the accompaniment of the newscaster's stream of words. He wakes up in the morning to the sound of another newscaster from the wireless set.

"Two trains have collided in India. A plane has crashed in Bolivia. An oil tanker has exploded in Turkey..."

Zinaida Stepanovna's kettle is boiling in the kitchen. She is Old Ma Utkina's daughter and the mother of Seryozha the schizophrenic.

She always takes her mother a cup of tea before she sets off to work.

Then she has to take the train, then the metro, and then a bus, to her workbench at the machine works.

Christlove goes into the communal kitchen.

"Morning, Zinaida Stepanovna," he says. "Zhurbin died in the night."

But Zinaida Stepanovna has no time for Zhurbin. She has enough problems of her own.

"Oh, Lord!" she sighs plaintively. "What have I done to deserve all this?! My son's a looney. My mother's almost off her rocker too. And I do nothing but work all day long. I can't go on like this. I'm sick to death of it. I've been waiting for a flat of my own for twenty years now. I don't believe I'll ever have my own kitchen. My own kitchen..." At this point Zinaida Stepanovna notices Christlove. "Oh, it's you."

"Yes, it's me," Christlove nods, feeling embarrassed for some reason that it is only him, Christlove.

"I used to take ballet lessons when I was a little girl, you know," Zinaida Stepanovna confides in him. "I dreamed of becoming a ballerina. You should have seen me dance..." She sighs again, plaintively. "Yesterday evening on the way from work I saw a notice in the metro: 'No way out'. See what I mean, Christlove. There's NO WAY OUT."

Christlove sees what she means all right. He trudges back to his room.

The wind howls miserably outside. "Oo-oo-oo."

Christlove sits down by the wireless set. The wireless set says to him:

"And now our coolest pop singer will sing you his latest hit recorded during his concert."

The song begins.

> *I love you!*
> *Dee-doo, dee-doo, dee-doo!*
> *And you love me!*
> *Dee-dee, dee-dee, dee-dee!*

"Now all together, please, everyone!" the coolest pop singer shouts.

The audience complies happily.

"Dee-dee, dee-dee, dee-dee!

Christlove joins in too:

"Dee-dee, dee-dee, dee-dee."

"And now it is time for our morning exercises." This is a different waveband. "We shall begin by marching on the spot. One, two, three! One-two-three!"

Christlove does the exercises. Squatting down, stretching to one side, shaking his wrists...

"Hop on your right leg. One-two-three-four. Now on your left leg. One-two-three-four."

Christlove hops. First on his right leg, then on his left. Trying his utmost.

"And now our last exercise. First we do a handstand against the wall..."

Panting hard, Christlove does a handstand against the wall. His head is a few inches above the floor.

"Now stretch out your arms!" the voice commands.

Christlove does as he is told and stretches out his arms.

"Ha-ha-ha!" the wireless set giggles. "So we end our early morning exercises with that schoolboy's joke. And now here's a modern arrangement of a waltz by old man Strauss."

Christlove lies concussed on the floor. Above him the room spins round with the 1957 wireless set emitting the strains of a Strauss waltz.

A Trip to Amsterdam

Translated by José Alaniz

Lately Kissin really felt like going to Amsterdam. But he'd kept putting it off. He didn't go in the winter, because he lacked sufficient spiritual fortitude not only for going to Amsterdam, but even for going to see a movie at the neighborhood cinema. And in the summer, well... in the summer he pretty much lacked sufficient spiritual fortitude, too. It was hot. Dusty. The train stations were packed with people.

"Russia just isn't my kind of place to live in," Kissin often reflected. "It's like a swamp here. It constantly drains me. If it's not one thing, it's another."

Engrossed in these thoughts, he once dropped by a small shop that sold ivory figurines. One of them struck his fancy.

"Would you please tell me what's the price on this one?"

"I'll tell ya," answered the fat-faced clerk. "but you gotta pay the cashier a grand for the info."

And Kissin understood: there was nowhere else to go. Only Amsterdam. At home he told his wife:

"Lena, I'm off to Amsterdam. Give me a couple of rubbers for the road."

"How about if I give 'em to you in the mouth?!" she replied.

Why did she answer me like that? wondered a stung Kissin, stamping towards the train station. And then he understood why. Because: she's a shit!

Amsterdam grew still more enticing.

At a payphone Kissin called his mistress, Shlyapnikova.

"Where've you been?" asked a displeased Shlyapnikova. "I've been lying naked here for a whole hour, like a piano."

"I'm leaving for Amsterdam," Kissin said importantly.

"Ooh, listen," his mistress started up. "Bring me back a fur coat and a pair of nice boots."

"Okay, fine, got it," said Kissin. "I have to go."

"Don't forget your little kitten!" cried Shlyapnikova by way of goodbye.

"What little kitten?" wondered a puzzled Kissin as he replaced the receiver.

He took his seat on the Amsterdam train at exactly 6 p.m. Interestingly, the carriage was empty. No one else wanted to go to Amsterdam. They were all fine right where they were.

In the compartment, besides Kissin, was a long-legged girl with luxurious hair. A train conductor with an inconsequential face checked their tickets; the locomotive gave a piercing whistle and... *they were off.* They trudged over cheerless Russian expanses.

To Amsterdam!

Soon dusk fell. The light came on in the compartment. Kissin opened a little illustrated magazine which he'd bought at the station, and engrossed himself in reading. Strangely enough, the short story which he'd opened at random was called "Beyond the Windows of a Night Train."

"On the night train, the lights had been extinguished," read Kissin, "the stifling air was steeped in gloom, the people were plunged into a deep slumber. I got up and opened the window — the night wind cooled my face. In the nocturnal murk, above a darkened plain, fireflies flew, doggedly flew, to some unknown destination. There they flew, their flight piercing the pitch darkness! Where was this train rushing in the middle of the moonlit night, to the accompaniment of the soft rumble of the wheels?" etc. etc.

Kissin got tired of reading, and took to looking out the window.

Suddenly the compartment door opened and the conductor

came in again. Standing in the passageway, he started recounting all his misfortunes, though nobody had asked him.

"I'm livin' a dog's life," said the conductor. "I started drinking and smoking. What can I do? My wife's sick. She's always depressed. I come home from work, she's sittin' there like a log on the couch. The kids ain't fed. Because 'a her, I'm a nervous wreck, too. I don't know what to do, I don't have the foggiest. Here I am workin' as a train conductor, with people. I have to be presentable all the time. But what kinda 'presentable' is this, if everything wears me out, if everything makes me tired..."

"You need a woman," said the long-legged girl. "On the side. To keep your spirits up."

"Easy for you to come up with that, 'on the side.' That's called *adultery*, when it's on the side." The conductor breathed a heavy sigh. "On top of that my brother hung himself last Sunday."

Kissin stared out the window. The train rumbled onward. Bushes, roads, far-away lights rushed by; they passed some dimly-lit railway stop with vague figures on its platform. Kissin imagined himself to be one of these figures when an Amsterdam-bound train tore by, and the wind whistled, and the wheels loudly rattled on the rails, and he so wanted to board that madly rushing train, to look out its window and ride and ride away...

In point of fact, Kissin *was* riding away.

Then staring out the window got boring too. He pointed his face back toward the compartment. The conductor was gone. The girl was sitting opposite Kissin, smoking an expensive cigarette. She had her long legs slightly parted. Kissin's gaze slid down... slid down some more...

And presto!... Presto!

Kissin gasped. His heart beat violently. The girl was wearing *see-through* panties.

Kissin was immediately seized with erotic desire, his mind was swimming. He sat next to the girl and stuck his palms into her luxurious tresses.

"I love every single one of your hairs," he whispered hotly, "every curl."

The girl "hmm"-ed indeterminately and pulled the wig off her head. She in fact had very short hair — almost a crew cut.

"Since you like them so much," she said, "You can have them."

Kissin was so shocked that his sexual ardor blew away like dust in the wind. Right then and there he found himself back in his rightful seat.

The girl produced a big red apple out of her bag and sunk her sharp teeth into it.

"Would you like a bite?" she asked Kissin.

Kissin thought the girl was giving him another apple, but she was only offering a bite.

He took a bite with a crunch. The apple was sour-sweet.

"What's your name?" he asked.

"Nora," the girl answered and took another bite of the apple.

"And where do you work?" Kissin further enquired.

"Nowhere. In general I don't believe that people should work."

"I'm a literary critic," said Kissin with importance. "I specialize in Pushkin."

Suddenly he was again fired up with piquant rapture at the thought that he had taken a bite of the apple from the girl's hands. "Like a dog!" Kissin mused with delight.

"Give me another bite," he asked, nodding to the apple.

Nora knowingly laughed out loud and extended the apple, already reduced nearly to a core. Kissin took a bite. His eyes shone.

"You know," he said, "Once, in kindergarten, I kissed a girl's foot. Even then I already had this complex: woman as mistress."

"*My* most vivid childhood memory is when I was blowing up condoms. Somebody had dumped a whole pile of used condoms into a trash pit. And we little kids got ahold of them and blew them up like balloons."

At this point the compartment door opened and once again the conductor with the inconsequential face came in.

"Do you know who I am?" he turned to the girl.

"I could, of course, be mistaken," said Nora, "but I think you're the conductor of this train."

"Nope," uttered the conductor with a scowl. "I am a third-class invalid. And any second I could be struck down by paralysis."

"Fascinating," said the girl, tossing the core under the table and starting to smoke again.

"Imagine a little party," the conductor went on. "Everybody's dancing. Me too. With her. She's pretty. I look her over from head to toe. Her breasts press up against my stomach. And I wanna... well, you know. To make a long story short, everything's great. Here we are in the middle of the room already, and instead of telling her, 'Your hips are so seductive,' and all that, I say, 'I am a third-class invalid. And any second I could be struck down by paralysis.' And that's it! It's over! Her eyes go all wide. She leaves me. She walks away. And the music keeps playing."

The girl shrugged. The conductor's story hadn't made the slightest impression on her.

"So what?" she said. "I, for instance, I've got fear of death syndrome. I'm always afraid I'm going to die."

"And I'm perfectly OK," Kissin blurted out for no reason, and immediately thought, "I shouldn't have said that."

"It's especially terrifying to die in good weather," continued Nora, not listening to him; then she paused, thought it over, and added, "though it's terrifying in bad weather, too."

Right on the tail of her last word, beyond the window rain poured down: onto the fields, the forests, the roads... in short, onto everything, including the train bound for Amsterdam!

"Russia's in the rain," pensively uttered Kissin, staring at tiny streams of water running down the glass.

"I'll bring some tea," said the conductor, and stepped out. But for some reason he returned not with tea, but a portable television set. He set it down on the table and turned it on. The screen resolved itself and there appeared a hot little announcer and next to her sat... Kissin.

"Whaddaya know," marveled the conductor, jabbing a finger at the screen. "That you they're showin' on the tube?"

"Yes," Kissin proudly assumed a dignified air. "That's me."

"Welcome to *Thoughts for the Day*," the hot little announcer was chirping. "Today our guest is the thought-manufacturer Kissin. Tell us, please, what thoughts have come into your head lately?"

Kissin — the one onscreen — also assumed a dignified air and answered:

"Well, just this week this idea occurred to me: life is death; death is life."

The hot little announcer beamed at this revelation.

"You're a genius! Dear friends, let's all reflect on the idea that this thought-manufacturer has so kindly communicated to us: *life is death; death is life!*"

As it turned out, Kissin had dozed off and it was just a dream.

He woke up. Beyond the window was a sunny day. Nora and the conductor were carrying on a literary discussion.

"I read some German dame here," the conductor was telling Nora. "Remarque was her name."

"Sure," nodded Nora. "Maria Remarque."

"Right, yeah. An' this is what she writes, the bitch... The hero there's a German, at the end of the book he frees some Russian prisoners from a camp. An' they kill him for that. Honestly."

Kissin felt rested and refreshed after his nap. He heartily split the air with his hand.

"I'm in the mood for a miracle!" he exclaimed. "I'm in the mood for the impossible... Like in a fairy tale. Elves, gnomes, fairies, enchanted castles, magic transformations... an extraordinary wonderful life. In our gray, drab existence, in spite of ourselves we're always waiting for something... like that. You wait and wait, and all of a sudden — it happens! You open a morning paper and find that you've been awarded the Nobel Prize."

"Me, in the morning I'm always looking for my right slipper," said the conductor. "For some reason it's always the right one that gets lost. You can't even imagine how much energy these searches take out of me. Makes me wanna kill myself. Honestly, I ain't lyin'."

"As for me," said Nora, languidly, "I get up in the morning, and I have to have a rest right after sleeping. I get so tired. That's why I start lunch right away. It's already past two, so what's the point of having breakfast. And again I have to rest, lie down, listen to music..."

The train screeched to a sudden halt. Nora and the conductor were thrown to the floor; Kissin hit his head painfully against the wall.

They had stopped in the middle of a forest. The twittering of birds was audible. The conductor went to see what was the matter. He soon came back.

"Some girl threw herself under the train," he reported. "Out of nothin' other than great love."

"Another Anna Karenina," said Nora contemptuously, making a wry face. "That's love for you," she continued, lighting a cigarette. "Love consists of tears, blood, violence, hatred, and finally, death.

And all the same a woman needs love more than anything," she threw a fleeting glance at Kissin. "Love, not sex."

"Did you know," Kissin suddenly remembered, "that according to the latest research it wasn't Tolstoy who wrote *Anna Karenina*, but some hooker who'd escaped from penal servitude."

"Aha! Aha!" the conductor triumphantly threw his pressed fist into the air. "I knew it! After all, there was no way a man could've described how a woman felt."

"Well, who knows," Kissin retreated at once. "The Russian soul is an enigma."

"No, it's not an enigma," said Nora in irritation. "If you opened it up, this famous Russian soul of yours, like a jar of preserves, it would turn out to be full of worms."

"Ugh," the conductor wrinkled up his face. "What're you talking about?"

"Yes! Yes!" Nora nodded excitedly. "Worms! Once I had a lover," she recalled with disgust. "A pathetic, push-over little queen. They're all so emotional. He'd write me love letters. And he'd sign them, 'Your Homosexual', meaning 'Intellectual'. With a capital 'I', naturally. And he was always late for our dates. He'd come after an hour and a half: 'Oh! Ah! Is it me you're waiting for?' Yes, you, you pederast."

The girl angrily stubbed out her unfinished cigarette.

Kissin fished Nora's still-smoking, lipstick-smudged cigarette out of the ashtray and dragged on it with pleasure.

"It seems you don't like men very much," he pointed out.

"I don't like women either," Nora clarified peremptorily. "I relate to them the same way I do to cockroaches — I can't believe such vile creatures exist!"

"What do you like, then?" asked the conductor.

"Fried chicken," Nora replied.

The train started up. And quickly gained speed. Soon the forest, the twittering birds, the girl suicide — all were left behind. In the past.

Kissin tried to find within himself even a grain of compassion for the dead girl, but couldn't. "The world is too huge," he thought in self-justification. "One person in it doesn't matter at all."

"I wouldn't be surprised if it turned out Pushkin didn't write his own stuff, either," the conductor continued the literary discussion, once the train had built up a comfortable speed; again they were on their merry way to Amsterdam, not stuck in the tedious backwoods of Russia.

"No way!" Kissin rose to Puskin's defense. "Everything having to do with Pushkin is on the up and up. I tell you this as a critic. True, his poetry isn't anything special. You know, it's as if some seductive little nymphet in a mini-skirt were walking by, and you trotted up and pulled her skirt up to her ass. And found nothing there! That's what Pushkin's verse is like: there's nothing there."

"And how do you feel about his prose?" asked Nora.

"Well, if I were to put it plainly," Kissin came completely unhinged, "then I'd say *it's crap!*"

After this lively outpouring the conversation quickly tapered off, and everyone took to staring out the window. The forest green was already noticeably tinged with yellow.

"There went summer," the girl sighed. "Now all that's left is to wait for winter... Then spring again... summer... fall..." And she sighed again. "In point of fact, this life of ours," Kissin said, following Nora's tone, "is a butterfly splattered on a windshield."

"Naah, it's more like... jumping without a parachute," the conductor chimed in melancholically.

Nora violently shook her head.

"This life of ours," she said curtly, as if putting down a period, "is a piece of shit. And that's it! And besides, the word 'ours' has no business here. There's nothing 'ours' about it. Everything belongs to God."

Kissin stood up, excused himself and went out into the passageway.

"You can use that newspaper in my compartment," the conductor yelled after him.

Kissin took the newspaper and sat his bare ass down on the toilet seat.

He started off reading a small notice under the headline "A Happy Accident" which caught his attention. It reported that a morgue worker had attempted sexual intercourse with a dead girl, who turned out not to be so dead after all. In the end he had to marry her, otherwise he would have been indicted for desecrating a corpse.

"A lucky break," thought Kissin, not sure himself whom he had in mind: the dead girl who turned up alive or the drunken rapist who wound up a bridegroom.

And suddenly!... Out of the blue!...

Kissin's hands shook. His mouth went dry. He waited for his violently racing heart to slow down a bit, and reread those lines, which quivered with excitement:

"...The Nobel committee awarded this year's Nobel Prize for Literature to the Russian author Valery Kissin. Oddly enough, the writer's name is unknown in Russia itself, even more so abroad. Why he was awarded the prize is quite incomprehensible."

The lavatory got a good rattle, and the newly-minted laureate collapsed onto the dirty floor.

Kissin was just daydreaming again.

He once more awoke. There was no trace of Nora or the conductor in the compartment. A little illustrated magazine lay on the table. Someone else's. The cover depicted a man with a red rose protruding from his neck instead of a head. The caption read: "In fashion this season: blooming men who blossom after dark."

Kissin opened the magazine at random and started to read:

"The city slept, as if all its citizens had imbibed some soporific and dozed off. At the same time, Stepan was dying.

'Stepan, dear,' tearfully pleaded Aglaya, 'don't die.'

'OK', answered Stepan and died."

Kissin leafed a few pages back, to the title. The story was called "The Death of Stepan."

The train came to a halt. Beyond the carriage window, Kissin saw wooden constructions of some sort, like barracks.

The compartment door opened. The conductor with the inconsequential face came in.

"Well?" he said. "We're here. The train doesn't go any farther."

Kissin stepped out onto a plank suburban platform. He saw an ancient hag in a shabby jersey and army boots. Near her stood a dirty skinny goat.

"Hullo, Granny," Kissin greeted her. "What station is this?"

"Amsterdam, what else," answered the hag.

My Flight to Malaysia

Translated by José Alaniz

Once I wrote a remarkable fairy tale and decided to take it to *Little Trolley*, a children's gazette. I walked into the editorial office, and sitting right there on the table was the editor, thoughtfully gazing at the ceiling.

"Just think," he was musing to himself, "how much free space that ceiling has. You could put a couch there, or a couple of armchairs, or even a television."

And here, as it turned out, was where I came in.

"Hello," I said. "I've written a new fairy tale."

"Yeah, so what?" the editor shrugged. "Are you going to order up a dance for the occasion?!"

And right then and there he jumped off the table and started dancing a fiery tap dance, then he performed a pas-de-deux from the ballet *Spartak*, and as a wrap-up he banged out some good old rock-n'-roll!

"Well, let's see your little fairy tale now," he said, panting slightly. "But not too close. There're mines all around this table. You'll blow up, and then I'll never hear the end of it."

I took the manuscript out of my pocket and showed it to him. The editor, to see better, perched his glasses on top of his nose and stretched out his neck. His neck seemed awfully long. Almost like a swan's.

"Well, well," he complimented me. "Outstanding paper, nice type face. We'll take it, of course. There's just one thing," he stopped short. "What do we do about the fee? You won't take money, will you?"

"No, I won't," I answered firmly. "Money spoils the writer."

"Y-up," he drawled out in thought, and started digging around in his numerous pockets in a fuss, turning them inside out. And what didn't he have in there: lighters, fountain pens, the *Family* magazine files for last year and next, half an apple, a short-barrel .34 caliber Colt, a glass eye, a live hamster named Phil, a raw chicken egg, a doughnut hole, an anti-tank grenade... and much else. Finally, he found what he was looking for. It was a crumpled plane ticket for a Boeing 747.

"Here," he held out the ticket to me. "In an hour you're flying to Malaysia. Seems to me that you're just what they need out there..." He thought a bit and held out the unfinished apple to me, too.

"Take an apple," he said, "for the road."

I took the apple and left for Malaysia. As soon as the Boeing 747 lifted off into the sky-blue sky, a pretty stewardess appeared, on such long legs that she had to bend down to keep from hitting her head on the ceiling.

"A good day to all our passengers," she said, smiling. "My name is Masha. Our flight today will be at an altitude of 6,000 meters. We're flying to Malaysia. The captain of our crew is pilot first class Ivan Potapov. He is a very experienced pilot. He's been in five air disasters and all five times he's made it through alive, when the other passengers and crew all perished. Have a pleasant flight, ladies and gentlemen. Thank you for your attention."

Then Masha the stewardess walked right up to me on her long legs.

"Excuse me," she asked. "Are you by any chance Hans Christian Andersen?"

"No," I admitted reluctantly, "my parents named me something else."

"But you do write fairy tales? Our pilot Potapov just adores

4*

fairy tales. As soon as he found out that you were on this flight, he wanted to meet you."

I walked up to the cockpit in the nose of the plane. There sat the pilot Potapov and two of his assistants. They were playing checkers. Give-away.

"A-a-a!!!" the pilot Potapov cried out, leaping up and hugging me hard to his mighty breast. "Hello, hello, Mister Andersen. I'm so glad to meet you. Potapov!"

"I'm very glad, too," I said. "But unfortunately, I'm not Andersen."

"How can this be?" he was a little stunned. "Wasn't it you who wrote *The Snow Queen*? And that story about that, what do you call it... that ugly duckling who lived on the roof."

"Alas, no," I sighed.

"Well, then, goodbye," the pilot Potapov coldly shook my hand. "If you see Andersen, give him my regards. Tell him like this: 'Potapov says he sends his regards.' "

And he sat down again to play give-away.

"Pardon my curiosity, but could you tell me who's more or less in charge of flying the plane?"

"Why, my son, Stepka," the pilot Potapov said from over his shoulder.

" 'Lemme steer, Papa,' he says, 'just a little bit.' Well, who am I to begrudge my only son? Steer to your heart's content!"

"You mean to say," I grew pale, "that the plane is being steered by a... kid?!"

"Kid? How do you like that!" harrumphed the pilot Potapov. "Next year he starts school. Kid! The lad's racked up five years already, so let him get used to being responsible for other people's lives. My Stepka has got 200 human lives in his hands!" Potapov the pilot said proudly. "Including, by the way, yours. And you say, 'kid.' "

I shook my head and started back to my seat. I had barely reached my seat when Masha the stewardess turned up again right next to me.

"I want to tell you the most curious piece of news," she whispered. "Our plane is going down."

"So what are you whispering to me for?" I replied, irritated. "That's not my business! Go to that Potapov of yours and whisper to him all you want!"

"Potapov and his crew have gone to sleep," said the stewardess. "They played give-away all night last night. They didn't get enough sleep. Now you couldn't wake them if you fired a cannon."

"What about Stepka?"

"He's crying. He's hungry."

"Well, give him some milk," I said.

"I don't have any," Masha sighed sadly. "Maybe you have some?"

I dug around in my pockets and pulled out the apple the editor had given me.

"Here," I said. "Take him this apple. Let him stuff himself."

Masha the stewardess walked off, but after a minute came back again.

"I gave it to him," she said. "That apple of yours. He gobbled it up and now he's asleep too."

"What do you mean asleep?!" I exclaimed. "He's got 200 human lives in his hands, including, by the way, mine!"

"Well, he's asleep," Masha answered. "What do you expect? The boy's only three years old."

"What do you mean only three years old?!" I was more amazed than before. "Potapov said he was five!"

"He added a couple of years, so the state commission wouldn't catch on and not let him fly airplanes. But, actually, he's three."

"O-o-o-o-o-okay," I'm thinking, "So tha-a-a-a-at's the deal..."
And meanwhile the other passengers are just sitting around: one's
reading a book, another one's munching sunflower seeds... And
the plane's GOING DOWN!!!

"Alright," I said to Masha. "Open up the entry hatch, and we'll
see where we're crashing."

She opened the hatch, grabbed me by the feet, and I hung
upside down out of the airplane. The wind was whistling in my
ears, the clouds rushing into my eyes... I got a good look, and
below us was... Malaysia. So we could go down with confidence.
What do you know, we'd made it...

"We're landing," I succinctly reported to Masha the stewardess
once she pulled me back into the plane.

And so we started our landing. Upon landing, we were met
by a black man. Black as coal, and very polite.

"Where is this," I asked him, "Malaysia?"

"As you say," he spread out his arms in greeting.

Masha the stewardess looked around and said, "This place
looks more like Polynesia to me."

"As you say," the black man spread out his arms in greeting
again.

"And who might you be?" I inquired. "Some local savage-
cannibal?!"

"Not at all," he replied. "I'm the president of this African republic,
Mister Matunta."

"So this is Africa!" I cried out in surprise.

"Absolutely right," the president nodded politely. "Therefore
I'd please like to welcome you to our Medical Center."

"Wh-what for?" I asked. "To get ourselves vaccinated or
something?"

"Not exactly," the president answered. "The thing is, here in

Africa everyone's black. So at the Center they'll take off your white hides and pull on black ones."

"Oh, how wonderful!" Masha the stewardess was delighted. "That means I'm going to be black!"

But for some reason I found the president's proposal not very appealing, or more truthfully, appealing, but not very, and even more truthfully, not appealing at all.

"Couldn't you just smear black paint on us?" I asked.

"But that would insult your human dignity," President Matunta shrugged his shoulders. "And besides, it's all very simple: they tear off your skin..."

"No, no," I hurriedly interrupted him. "You know, we're used to insults. So please go ahead and insult us — paint us black."

President Matunta right then and there fetched some oil paint and, with a brush, painted us black.

"Well, there you go, Mr Ronshin. You're black," he said to me. "Congratulations."

"Huh?" I was surprised. "You know me?!"

"Sure, here in Africa every macaque knows you," laughed the president. "You're the one who wrote this:

> *Children, don't go to Africa to play!*
> *There're gorillas, mean crocodiles, in Africa!*
> *In Africa there's the monster BAR-MA-LEI!!!*

"Yes," I said jokingly, "I wrote that." (In fact, it was from a poem by Chukovsky, but sometimes, you know, it's nice to bask in someone else's fame.) As I uttered these words, I was taken into custody by two guards who looked just like those same gorillas from "my" poem.

"You're under arrest," President Matunta said tenderly.

"What for?!" I cried out.

"For these very verses. Because of them tourists, along with their children, have stopped coming to Africa. They're afraid of mean crocodiles and the Barmalei. So, if you don't write a retraction right this minute... I'll eat you!"

You can well imagine, I wrote a retraction right then and there:

> *Children, come on over to Africa to play!*
> *The mosquitoes fly around on little air balloons,*
> *And you'll meet your kindly uncle Bar-ma-lei!!!*

"Now this is something else, indeed," President Matunta praised me, and then he named me editor-in-chief of an African children's magazine, *Young Cannibal.* Masha the stewardess and I got married, and soon after a black stork brought us a little black girl, who (when she grew up) married Stepka, the son of the pilot Potapov.

Potapov himself began writing fairy tales and signed them "Hans Christian Andersen." At which the editor of *Little Trolley* remarked, "Potapov, if you're Andersen I'm a Boeing 747." The pilot Potapov was very insulted and stopped reading *Little Trolley.* But who cares.

One Cloudy Day

Translated by Edmund Glentworth

In a small provincial town there lived a true Russian intellectual by the name of Karmalyutov. His world was very rich in spirit. For example, he could down ten bottles of vodka in one go. And not die.

But, of course, like every true Russian intellectual he had his eccentricities. Karmalyutov always walked about in a gas mask. And ate in a gas mask. And slept in a gas mask.

And even got married without taking off his gas mask because his beloved Dasha was also a true intellectual. She had no interest in material things. She was attracted to Karmalyutov's rich spiritual world.

Often in the evenings, Dasha would gaze into her husband's eyes and exclaim:

"You are an angel. A pure angel."

"Calm down, Dasha. Stop it!" Karmalyutov slapped her across the face.

But his blows only drove her to deeper passion.

"No, no, don't speak. Oh, your eyes! My god, what eyes you have. So round and shiny."

She would start to have real hysterics. She would leap about frenetically, ripping her clothes off.

"Now I'm going to make dumplings," Dasha would mutter as if in a trance.

She would fly naked to the kitchen.

"Where are you going?" Karmalyutov wondered.

"To make dumplings."

Within a minute she would return all covered in cream sauce.

"So?" proffering her plump breasts.

"Delicious," Karmalyutov would answer, greedily licking her from head to foot.

Then they would simply lie down in bed and talk.

"A woman is a sandwich," Karmalyutov announced portentously.

"What shall I wear in winter?" Dasha replied. "I don't have a fur coat, not even of fake fur."

"If you like, I'll buy you a fake cock, a dildo," suggested Karmalyutov after a moment's thought.

"I don't need a cock," Dasha spat with irritation, "I need a fur coat."

"How can you even talk about such things?" Karmalyutov was getting angry. "What kind of devils have got into you?"

"What things?" asked Dasha nonplussed.

"Well, you know — fur coats... what shall I wear in winter."

"So what shall I wear in winter?"

Karmalyutov shut his eyes, utterly drained of strength.

"Well, what did Fyodorov wear?" he asked weakly.

"Which Fyodorov? Jee-eesus!"

"Our philosopher of genius, who always wore a tattered old overcoat. And died, note, from the care of friends. There was a sharp frost and his friends wrapped him in a fur coat. He caught cold, contracted pneumonia and died. And he'd still be walking around in his tattered old overcoat with his organs still functioning; you see — he'd still be alive."

"Oh go to hell!" yelled Dasha and turned away to the wall.

"It is necessary to suffer," Karmalyutov began to lecture to her back. "To suffer, yes. You should understand, Dasha, that you lead a bad life. I lead a bad life too. But my life is morally better than yours, because of how much I suffer."

"I don't want to suffer," thought Dasha miserably, looking at a cockroach climbing up the wall. "I want pleasure. I want to be pleasured by a man," she confided to herself. "Or two men," she confided further. "Well, better make it three."

Karmalyutov reached out and turned on the television, which was showing some kind of trashy film.

"What is this trash?" growled Karmalyutov looking at the screen. Then louder: "Trash! Trash! Trash!" He looked again at Dasha's back, and his eyes suffused with blood. "Trash!" thundered Karmalyutov. "You're trash!!!" He shook.

Outside in the wind the leaves were rustling furiously, and a heavy rain began to fall.

"Autumn," thought Karmalyutov, having calmed down in an instant. "Autumn... Autumn..." His heart at once softened.

"Hey," dreamily putting his hands behind his head. "How good it would be to fart off and fly away."

Dasha turned from the wall.

"I've never seen your face. Why, oh why, do you always go about in a gas mask?"

"I'm in mourning for my life," replied Karmalyutov sadly. "I am unhappy. Remember last week I went to Tula. In principle I felt as though I could have been in, say, Paris. People everywhere, shops everywhere, regardless of whether they have anything to sell or not. A chemist is always a chemist, a shithole is always a shithole."

"Alright then," Karmalyutov suddenly resolved. "Look!"

He ripped the gas mask from his head. Dasha gazed in silence.

"Well?" asked Karmalyutov impatiently.

"You have a face like a dead man," she pronounced thoughtfully. "I can't explain it, but..." Dasha searched for the right definition. "Corpses' faces are just as weird. Bloated."

Karmalyutov's good mood vanished like the wind. He got out of bed and went to the bathroom. He splashed some water on his face and pissed in the basin. In the kitchen Karmalyutov poured himself a whole bowl of cabbage soup and began to slurp it greedily.

"The world is full of mud, blood and sperm," he thought munching on some cabbage.

Unexpectedly, Karmalyutov saw his naked body as if from outside. White, flaccid and gangly. It revolted him. He forced down his soup without any appetite. On the bottom of the empty bowl lay a pair of nail scissors.

"I am mad," muttered Karmalyutov staring at the scissors. "Yes, I'm mad. Only you'll never make me admit it." He laughed out loud. "Ha ha ha..."

Lying in the dark room under the blanket and listening to the sound of rain mingled with the wild laughter of Karmalyutov, Dasha thought: "Tomorrow I'll have to call a vet."

The next day a vet arrived with the suspicious name of Pissoff. He limped on both legs and was thin as a rake.

"Would you like some tea?" Dasha offered.

"I would not," said the vet. "But you may pour some anyway."

They sat down to drink tea and immediately started arguing about the secrets of the universe.

"When I look at a woman I think that before me must be revealed the secrets of the universe," said Karmalyutov hotly, "but all I see, sorry, is a pussy."

"Karmalyutov," Dasha winced, "don't be vulgar."

"Mustn't look at it, old chap," the vet Pissoff expostulated, "but through it. Because then it'll lead you to the secrets of the universe".

Dasha was visibly aroused. She licked her lips greedily.

"It's time to make dumplings," flashed through her mind.

"You know," continued Pissoff sipping his tea, "in my spare time I teach at a Yoga Centre. One day a woman came up to me.

Not so young any more. `I want to fly,' she said. `I love height. That's why I chose to work as a crane operator' ".

"And what did you say to her?" asked Karmalyutov with interest.

"I replied that flying could only be learned by flying. So she jumped straight out of the window. From the twelfth floor."

"And then what?" asked Dasha in shock.

"She flew away," said Pissoff emphatically.

"Impossible!" gasped Dasha.

"But she did," stated Pissoff portentously. "You must understand, my friends, that man is not at all what we see. If you don't wash him for a month, don't let him cut his hair or clean his teeth then you'll see him for what he is."

There was a silence.

"What a cloudy day," said Dasha pensively, looking out of the window. "It'll surely rain today."

Just then it began to pour.

"So what is to be done?" asked Karmalyutov, shivering.

"In what sense?" asked Pissoff.

"Metaphysically," explained Karmalyutov.

"Nothing can be done," answered Pissoff and yawned. "As with everything, it is much more simple and much more complicated. Simultaneously. What is the thing you most dislike in life?"

Karmalyutov wrinkled his brow.

"In principle," he conceded, "I don't like anything in life. But the thing I loathe most is when a dog licks someone's gob off the ground. The sight of it simply makes my stomach churn."

"There I very well understand you," said the vet nodding. "Oftentimes I say to God: Lord, let go! Lord, let go!"

"And what does He do?" asked Dasha.

"He does not let go."

There was another silence. Meanwhile, the rain had stopped. The vet Pissoff gazed absently out the window. His gaze fell on Karmalyutov. Only now did he notice that Karmalyutov was in a gas mask.

"Why are you wearing a gas mask?" asked Pissoff. "What's up? Have you got a leak from the gas oven?"

"And why do you limp on both legs?" Karmalyutov answered his question with a question. "Are you an old sea wolf?"

"As a child I suffered from tuberculosis of the bones," explained Pissoff.

"And in my childhood I was poisoned by my mother's milk," sniggered Karmalyutov.

"Don't understand," frowned the vet and looked at Dasha.

"What do you think of when you look at me?" Dasha interjected with an apologetic half-smile.

"Orange juice in a tall glass," smiled Pissoff.

"And you, Karmalyutov?" she addressed her husband.

"Muddy old boots," Karmalyutov barked maliciously.

"You see," sighed Dasha.

"Why am I here?" once more Pissoff was at a loss. "I am a vet."

"So put him to sleep," said Dasha. "Like a dog."

"You're a real trooper," exclaimed Pissoff. "You come straight to the point."

He got a syringe out of his bag and gave Karmalyutov a shot. Karmalyutov fell silent. Outside it started raining again.

"Dasha," Karmalyutov whispered. "I am dying."

"So what? What do you expect me to do?" Dasha shrugged.

"Dasha, shut the window. I'm feverish."

Dasha shut the window, and having returned to her place could no longer restrain her curiosity.

"Is it frightening to die?"

Karmalyutov looked at his wife through half-closed eyes.

"No," he said with difficulty. "It is not frightening to die. Everything else is frightening."

The vet Pissoff rattled his bag loudly.

"Well," he said. "Time for me to go. I have three more calls today. Thank you very much for the tea."

"Maybe you could express your thanks in some other way?" Dasha was disappointed.

"Goodbye," bowed Pissoff. "Don't forget God."

And the vet left. Dasha drained the remains of his tea, deriving a strange pleasure from it, and thought about God. "The world is full of love, warmth and light," she thought, looking at Karmalyutov who had been put to sleep. Then she opened a volume of Nabokov and buried herself in reading. A few years passed. Karmalyutov had never woken up. Dasha married again, either a policeman or a waiter, more likely both at once. It was essential for her to have someone to care for; she could not live just for herself. Soon she died in childbirth. The vet Pissoff changed his name to Pissupoff. One day he was walking past a pond, slipped in and drowned. To live in Russia is hard, but to die is dead easy. Why this should be, I do not know.

Zaborov the Dreamer

Translated by Sofi Cook

Zaborov the dreamer liked to fly around in the clouds and dream his dreams. Zaborov's neighbour, a retired colonel who could see right through anyone, didn't approve at all.

"I've no time for all this flying around," he used to say. "Someone has to do the work, don't they?"

This didn't stop Zaborov though. He would soar high up above, like a bird. And quite often he would shout down in a burst of delight: "People, I love you all!"

The people, however, all tended to be like his neighbour, the colonel. Whenever they spotted Zaborov the dreamer soaring in the sky, they would throw stones at him, or fire their shotguns in order somehow to bring him back to earth.

One day, as Zaborov was flying over a military unit, they tried to bring him down with a burst of machine-gun fire.

"Well, what did you expect?" said his neighbour, the colonel, who could see right through anyone. "Every Soviet is a KGB man at heart. Here you are flying around without anyone's authorization! We can't have that, you know! What if everyone suddenly took it into their heads to start flying around? Who would do all the work around here then, eh?!"

After this Zaborov the dreamer stopped flying.

"Good lad," his neighbour exclaimed approvingly. "Now all you need to do is get a job, and start being of some use to society."

Zaborov the dreamer did not become of any use to society, however. He took to visiting the town park, where he would lie on the grass and watch the clouds go by. Yet even this did not last long. One day, he was approached by a policeman.

"What do you think you're doing, lying around, then, eh?" inquired the policeman.

"I'm watching the clouds," replied Zaborov the dreamer.

"And why is that?" inquired the policeman again.

"Well, I just feel like it," replied Zaborov the dreamer.

"Perhaps you should come with me then," retorted the policeman.

At the police station Zaborov the dreamer had to make a statement and was fined for unruly behaviour in a public place.

After this Zaborov the dreamer stopped lying in the park and watching the clouds.

Winter came, and one day Zaborov the dreamer was walking along a sleety street, looking carefully underfoot so as not to fall, when suddenly by the Intourist Hotel he bumped into his childhood flame and first love, Nadenka. The two used to go to nursery school together.

Now Nadenka worked as a prostitute, for foreign currency only. She invited Zaborov the dreamer to a nice restaurant.

"Still flying around?" she asked, sipping her champagne.

"Do you remember how we used to roll about in the snow?" reminisced Zaborov, smiling. "Those huge white snowdrifts!"

"No," replied Nadenka. "No, I don't remember."

"And in the summer we used to go down to the river. Remember when you got that fisherman to let you have the fish he'd caught which you let go?"

Nadenka didn't remember any of this.

"I'm worth three hundred dollars now, you know," she boasted.

Zaborov touched her hand timidly. His soul wept for her.

When Zaborov the dreamer returned home his neighbour, the colonel, who could see right through anyone, immediately saw through his soul.

"I suppose she's been snivelling again?" he sneered.

"I shall fly again today," Zaborov said quietly.

"Idiot!" shouted the colonel.

But Zaborov the dreamer flew away anyway. He floated quietly above the sleeping earth and dreamed his dreams: "Wouldn't it be wonderful if all people could learn to take away each other's pain. And share their joy in return."

Zaborov the dreamer was so full of his dream that he didn't even notice the intercepting fighter plane heading straight towards him. In the cockpit sat a fighter pilot whose code number was "Nineteen".

"I see the target!" Nineteen reported to his command post.

"Destroy!" came the order.

"Yes, sir!" replied Nineteen and destroyed Zaborov the dreamer. With an "air-to-air" missile.

How I Became a Fly

Translated by Sofi Cook

Once upon a time there lived little me. And, one fine day, there I was, as usual, standing behind the counter of my little shop. Outside the sun shone brightly. A fly was buzzing around the room. In short, everything was just as usual. All of a sudden, the door opened and a strange customer walked in. Or rather, he wasn't strange — until he began to speak.

"I would like to buy a heart," he said.

"In that case, you should try the shop next door," I suggested. "I'm afraid we don't sell toys."

"You misunderstand me," the strange customer insisted gently. "I wish to buy a real, live heart."

"I'm sorry," I said, "but we don't sell anything like that."

"I'll pay you well," he insisted, pulling a thick wad of notes out of his pocket.

"But I don't have any live hearts in my shop!" I exclaimed. "You may buy a typewriter, or a television — anything down to a box of matches!"

"No, no," the strange customer retorted firmly. "I need a heart. Your heart."

"Mine?" I gaped in astonishment.

"Yes, yours," he nodded calmly.

"Well, I'm afraid you're wasting your time," I concluded. "My heart is not for sale."

"I do understand," agreed the stranger. "Of course you won't sell it cheaply. But if I were to offer you a very substantial sum..?"

Upon which he pulled a second wad of money from his pocket. It was three times as thick as the first.

I gazed thoughtfully at the notes lying on the counter.

"But... how will I live without a heart?" I ventured falteringly. "It's impossible!"

"It's perfectly possible," the stranger disagreed. "Think of all the people who do!"

Saying this, he stretched his black gloved hands towards me and his fingers entered my chest as though it were water. In an instant my red heart lay in his palms. Whereupon the strange customer took a soiled plastic bag from his pocket, smoothed it out and carelessly threw my pulsating heart into it.

"See you," he uttered meaningfully as he disappeared behind the door.

My chest now felt light and airy. I pounced on the notes to count them again.

The next day the stranger appeared for a second time.

"Are you looking for another heart?" I asked. "I'm afraid I don't have another one."

"Ah, but you do have a brain," he grinned unpleasantly.

Involuntarily I put my hand to my head.

"A brain," I whispered hesitantly. "But... what will I think with?"

"Why think at all?" riposted the stranger.

"How much?" I inquired, business-like.

"Enough, never you worry," he answered, taking three fat wads from his pocket.

And then he plunged his fingers into my head and took out my brain.

We stared at it for a minute. To tell the truth, there didn't seem to be that much grey matter. Getting out another dirty plastic bag, the strange customer threw my brain in it and withdrew.

I immediately counted the money. The sum really was very substantial. And now my head, as well as my chest, felt light and airy.

On the third day I found myself awaiting the arrival of the mysterious stranger with impatience. He did not disappoint my expectations and appeared in due course.

"Good afternoon," he said politely. "And how are you feeling today?"

"Wonderful!" I enthused. "My head is no longer crammed full of utter rubbish. Perhaps you would like to purchase something else?" I suggested hopefully.

"Your right leg," the stranger said curtly.

My jaw dropped.

"And I'll just hop, I suppose?" I inquired sarcastically.

"What for?" he shrugged disdainfully. "Just stand still."

Saying this, he was already pulling the money from his pocket.

"You'd convince a dead man!" I surrendered, and continued with abandon: "Well, in for a penny, in for a pound! Take both legs!"

To cut a long story short, pretty soon I had sold him everything: my arms, legs, torso, liver and spleen, — even my bladder! Only my head, emptied of its brains, remained sitting on the counter. This he didn't even think was worth talking to, and simply flung it in his dirty plastic bag before departing.

My soul alone was left in the shop.

Imagine my astonishment, when the following day the strange visitor appeared again!

"You would like to buy my soul?" I asked.

"What would I want with your soul?" he grimaced disdainfully. "No, give me a box of matches."

"What can I give it to you with?" I asked, a little surprised. "Remember, you bought my hands a good week ago! You might as well just help yourself."

He took a box of matches and lit up, quite unruffled.

"How would you like to become a fly?" he asked unexpectedly.

"A fly?" I repeated.

"You know — a fly," the stranger nodded. "Then you can fly around the lamp, buzzing away to yourself. Come on — see if you can buzz a little!"

"Buzzzzzzzzz," I buzzed obligingly.

"See how good you are," he concluded in negligent praise.

And so I became a fly.

We All Lived... We All Loved

Translated by Sofi Cook

Mum rang towards evening. She told me that grandfather had died. I went back into the other room. The first drops of rain were falling on the window pane.

"It's raining," Vika said.

When I first met Vika she was lying on my friend's sofa, eyes half-closed, reading a poem:

"Blue people walk among the red..."

Now Vika lay on my sofa.

Grandfather had lived for fifty-two years before I was born. A whole lifetime. What did I really know about him?

"Why don't you put some music on," said Vika. "You know silences disturb me."

We would come and visit every summer. Grandfather would water the vegetable garden with the hose, breed rabbits, and mess around with his motor-scooter in the shed. What else? Read the papers.

Now he was dead.

> *"All men are brothers,*
> *But we're cousins many times removed.*
> *And we're travelling somewhere,*
> *not knowing where and why!"*

— blared the music from the speakers.

At the very moment grandfather was dying I was kissing Vika's breasts.

"Darling," she was whispering in my ear, "when are we going to go to the registry office?" Vika badly wanted to get married.

Instead, she got hit by a tram. There you are, you see. You want one thing and you get another. Outside it was drizzling.

> *"My neighbour can't take it,*
> *he wants to escape*
> *But he can't get away —*
> *he does not know the way."*

Sorrowfully, Jesus Christ gazed down at us from the icon in the corner. Night was falling. From the gathering shadows the midges flocked to the light of the lamp.

"He wanted you to come so much," grandmother had said, "but you never came."

Our cold tea stood untouched in the cracked teacups.

The next morning I went for a walk around the town. Not much had changed.

Beside the old maternity hospital where I had been born there now stood a new hospital where grandfather had died.

And you could now go on a bus tour around the town.

"The writer Gogol stayed in our town," commented the young guide. "Now, if you look to your right..."

Everyone looked to their right.

The cemetery fence had collapsed in places. The photograph on the iron tombstone was the same as the one in the little frame in the kitchen. Was it really possible that my grandfather was buried here? Strange idea. I couldn't imagine it. I just kept on hearing his voice in my head.

Four men were carrying a nailed-down coffin along one of the little paths. Another eight or so people followed. An old woman in black had to be supported on either side.

"If you die this year, you can't die next year!" winked the man who brought up the rear, a little drunk.

In the bus someone had scratched on the back of the front seat: "Is this how we should be living?"

The guide, whom I knew, was sitting to my left. Turning to face him I asked:

"Why was it that Gogol stayed in this town?"

"His carriage had broken down," he replied.

The bus left a long trail of dust. Somewhere a dog barked. The rather tatty "unknown soldier" kept his lonely vigil by the eternally dying flame. The bus drove onto the main square, where the plywood stands were ablaze with figures: rows and rows of red numbers showing our achievements.

Brezhnev stared pompously at himself from three huge posters. The sun was setting. I thought of Vika.

"I suppose I'd better go now," she had said, not moving.

"'Bye then," I had replied.

"You pig," she had said.

Sitting in my armchair I could hear Vika in the hall as she put her coat on. The door slammed. Where was she now — my first love? And where was the guide who had talked about Gogol? And where was Gogol himself — Gogol, who wrote "Living is a dull business, gentlemen"? Where's the unknown soldier? And that well-known Leninist, Leonid Brezhnev? Where is Jesus Christ, who said, "Save us, o Lord!" Where are they all, I would like to know? And where, indeed, am I myself? So clever! So handsome! And so unique!

Doctor Gogol

Translated by Sofi Cook

Once upon a time there lived a doctor, whose surname was that of the greatest Russian writer. That is to say, Gogol. Doctor Gogol was rather a strange chap. One day, for instance, a pretty young girl came to see him.

"Oh, Doctor Gogol," she wept. "I've trapped my finger in the door."

"We'll have to amputate," Gogol snapped curtly, not even glancing at the finger.

"My f-finger?" the young girl stammered, white as a sheet.

"Your hand!" the doctor replied firmly.

Crash! — the young girl fainted.

One day Doctor Gogol had a rather strange idea. He decided to go to the cemetery where his namesake was buried and dig up his coffin to see what exactly remained of the great Russian writer.

So off he went, armed with a spade. At the cemetery he dug up the grave, opened the coffin, and...

There was no-one inside!

It was totally empty.

"Hmm," pondered Gogol. "I wonder where the writer could have got to." Then he had another idea: "Why don't I lie down in his place just to see what lying in a grave's like!"

So he got in the coffin, closed the lid and lay still.

Just then an old drunkard was passing through the cemetery. Seeing an unburied coffin, he said to himself: "This ain't right!" — and buried Doctor Gogol.

And so there was Gogol the doctor lying in the coffin of Gogol the writer, marvelling at the vicissitudes of life: an hour ago he had

been at home, happily eating dumplings with sour cream, and now he was lying in a grave in the middle of a cemetery. Six feet under.

So he lay there and marvelled, until finally he nodded off.

Now it so happened that at the same time, some scholars from the Academy of Sciences also decided to dig up the coffin with the remains of the writer Gogol. With a scientific aim in mind, of course.

So they dug up the coffin, took it to the Academy of Sciences, put it on a table and carefully opened it.

And there was Doctor Gogol, fast asleep.

Astonished, the scholars gathered around the coffin.

"Gracious!" they said.

"Isn't the body remarkably well-preserved!"

One professor named Paukin ventured to express some doubt, however.

"Wasn't Gogol's nose rather pointed?" he asked timidly. "This chap's got a snub nose. And also Gogol always wore his hair long — and this one's bald as a coot."

The other scholars soon brought him to reason.

"What do you expect?" they screeched. "The body's been buried for years! Of course there'd be a few slight changes!"

At this point Doctor Gogol awoke, climbed out of the coffin and jumped down onto the tiled floor.

"Greetings, my good men," he said.

The learned scholars were gobsmacked.

"So he didn't die at all," they whispered. "He was just in a coma."

Academician Vasilenko, president of the Academy of Sciences, inquired politely:

"How are you feeling, Mr Gogol?"

"Well enough," replied Doctor Gogol.

"Can I get you anything?" Vasilenko offered invitingly.

"Some vodka might be nice!" said Doctor Gogol.

The vodka was brought immediately. Doctor Gogol had a drink and livened up.

"Now bring me a woman!" he shouted.

"I still say there's something funny about him," insisted Professor Paukin.

"What do you expect?" the others came down on him again. "All those years without a woman! It's a perfectly natural wish!"

By now Doctor Gogol had got completely out of hand and was bawling: "Get me a woman! I want a woman!"

There was nothing for it but to get him a woman.

The woman was Nastasia Petrovna, the cleaner. Now Nastasia Petrovna was a large woman. People say of women like her, "She could give birth to a tank and the tank crew."

The professors and academicians retired tactfully to another room. Doctor Gogol remained staring at Nastasia Petrovna. He couldn't believe his eyes: could this really be Nastenka, that same Nastenka he had had such fun with twenty years ago?

"Nastenka!" he growled in disbelief. "Is it you?"

"Grigory!" gasped Nastasia Petrovna.

"Dear Nastenka!" reminisced Doctor Gogol sentimentally. "What's happened to you, my dear? Remember — you used to write poetry! *Come, oh come, our souls are pining. In the heavens the stars are shining.*"

"I did," Nastenka agreed, "and now I clean toilets. You're not so fine either, Grigory: remember when you used to rush to your lectures, a fresh-faced young student — and look at you now! They pulled you out of a coffin like a dead'un!"

"Indeed, my dear, indeed," Doctor Gogol shook his bald head sadly. "Life is a strange thing."

Round about this time the scholars, encouraged by their first success, decided to nip up to the Pushkin Hills and dig up the coffin of Alexander Pushkin in the vague hope that he had not been killed in the duel, but had also fallen into a coma.

So they dug up the coffin, took it to the Academy of Sciences, put it on a table and, not without considerable trepidation, opened it.

Inside lay a woman, blind-drunk. She looked around with a dull expression, heaved herself up into a sitting position, letting her legs dangle from the table, and inquired sullenly:

"Where am I then? In the nick?"

"You are in the Academy of Sciences," announced the scholars.

"Blimey," she retorted indifferently and hiccoughed.

"Excuse me, madam," Academician Vasilenko questioned her, "but who exactly are you?"

"Don't know," shrugged the woman and hiccoughed again.

"Madam, I must insist," Vasilenko continued coldly, "that you tell me how you came to be in the coffin of Alexander Pushkin."

"Can't remember, shit!" snapped the old bag and blew her nose into her fingers. "I remember I bought a bottle with the boys, and I remember we drank it in the alley by the skip, but I don't remember nothin' else. Passed out, didn't I!"

The learned scholars were somewhat taken aback. And indeed, the situation was rather odd: no Pushkin — just some old alkie in his place. What was going on?

Suddenly the silence was broken by a very perturbed Professor Paukin.

"She's my wife," he confessed hoarsely. "Her name's Emma. She's a chronic alcoholic."

"That's right!" the old bag brightened up. "I'm his wife I am! 'Cause my husband's a clever sod — he's a professor he is! How could I forget that?"

"I thought you said your wife was a ballerina," Academician Vasilenko began sternly. "Now it turns out she's a chronic alcoholic."

"Well I got muddled up," Paukin sighed in contrition.

Taking Nastasia Petrovna's arm, Doctor Gogol intervened: "We're leaving. Goodbye."

The scholars all rose up in alarm.

"But, Mr Gogol, why leave so soon?"

"Wait, Mr Gogol, please wait!"

The doctor looked round.

"I make about as good a Gogol as she makes a Pushkin," he retorted, pointing at Emma.

And this was only the beginning.

In Leo Tolstoy's coffin they discovered Peter Titkin, the plumber at housing office No 14 in Kazan. He swore dreadfully, and even bit Professor Paukin on the thigh.

Instead of Anna Akhmatova they discovered Klavka Zudova the beer seller, whose nickname was "Slut". She was forty-three and single, but had chalked up twelve abortions.

In Alexander Blok's grave they found the sex maniac Makarov, for whom the police had hitherto searched in vain.

And as for Fyodor Dostoyevsky — well, the story is really rather embarrassing. You see, when they dug up his large, old-fashioned coffin in the Alexander Nevsky cathedral and opened it, they found a stark naked girl, making love with two men at once. Furthermore, one of these two men was none other than Academician Vasilenko who had, just the day before, allegedly departed on urgent business to the Kuril Islands.

Living is a dull business, gentlemen.

How Tryapkin the Detective Set out to Moscow and Arrived in Arsehole

Translated by Sofi Cook

Once upon a time there lived a detective named Tryapkin. One day the detective Tryapkin received an order from a very important general to go and see him. Or rather, her — since the general was a woman, Maria Petrovna.

"Tryapkin," she began, adjusting her mighty general's bosom under her uniform. "Tryapkin, I would like to entrust you with a most unusual case."

"Yes, general," Tryapkin moved closer to show his readiness to serve.

"All our passenger trains travelling from Petersburg to Moscow have begun simply to disappear! What is more, they disappear without a trace, Tryapkin — without a trace!"

"What do you mean — `they disappear'?" Tryapkin inquired in bewilderment.

"That's up to you to find out!" concluded Maria Petrovna the general. "You're not a detective for nothing, are you now?"

So off went Tryapkin to the railway station, to find out.

He bought a ticket, boarded the train and was soon on his way to Moscow.

"Now, I must be on the look-out," said Tryapkin to himself, and he stayed awake all night waiting for mysterious terrorists to attack. But no-one attacked him at all.

The night passed, morning came, and still no-one had hijacked the train.

In fact, here was Moscow! The loudspeaker announced: "Ladies and gentlemen, our train has now arrived in Moscow. Please check your documents and belongings to make sure that you have not been robbed during your journey. Goodbye."

So Tryapkin and all the other passengers got off the train and started to walk down the platform. Tryapkin's keen detective's sense told him that something was wrong, however. Everything appeared to be right — and because everything appeared to be right, Tryapkin felt there had to be something wrong.

There were the long-distance trains and there were the suburban trains. There was the big digital clock showing the time, and there were the passengers making their way towards the station with their luggage.

And then suddenly Tryapkin understood what was the matter!

There was no-one there to meet them! And there was no-one there seeing anyone off! And, in fact, there was no-one leaving to be seen off. Actually, there didn't seem to be anyone there at all! The place was deserted.

Just the passengers plodding towards the station. Plod-plod. Plod-plod.

Tryapkin followed them, of course. Though he had a most unpleasant feeling in his stomach, as if he'd eaten a live mouse or drunk some prussic acid.

They neared the station doors, and Tryapkin's heart sank. For this was no station — it was simply a plywood wall, made to look roughly like a station. The digital clock was only painted. In short, it was basically a stage set.

Behind this wall, as far as the eye could see, stretched an unearthly landscape: a brownish soil without a single blade of grass and a brown cloudless sky. And so right up to the very horizon. Above the horizon there hung two black suns.

And it was full of cockroaches. Cockroaches, cockroaches, cockroaches — the place was teeming with them. Not just little ones either, but the size of a good cow.

Brown ones, with long feelers, who ordered everyone in flawless Russian:

"Lay down your luggage to your right! Go round to your left! Hands behind your backs! Get into groups of five! Don't mill around like sheep!"

The former travellers obeyed without a murmur. Nobody seemed too surprised at this turn of events: they were used to everything. Certainly, obeying orders was no novelty. Hands behind their backs, they arranged themselves in groups of five and off they marched across the brown earth and beneath the brown sky.

The cockroaches marched alongside.

Tryapkin the detective found himself beside the biggest cockroach of all, who was evidently in charge of the rest.

"Tell me, my friend," Tryapkin inquired amicably, "how are we to understand this? And where are we?"

"In Deepest Arsehole," answered the cockroach.

"And where are we going?" Tryapkin asked again.

"Where you always were going," replied the cockroach, pointing a furry leg at the two black suns. "Towards the Radiant Future!"

A day went by, then two. Another month passed, then a whole year. And still they all dragged dejectedly on like so many dead men. All of them — or not quite all.

"Serve us idiots right!" a bearded old man in a Russian shirt shouted cheerfully. "The cockroach is an intelligent animal, not like some old louse or bedbug!"

Soon people in the crowd began to volunteer to help drive the crowd on. They would approach the cockroaches deferentially and offer their services. The cockroaches had no scruples about allowing this. And soon the column were flanked by people as well as cockroaches, cracking their whips in the air and shouting: "Look lively there, lads! Don't lag behind!"

As the column reached the top of a hill, Tryapkin looked around and his jaw dropped. The whole of Russia was there.

EVERYONE!!!

Every single Russian was present, like in that Glazunov painting. And there, indeed, was old Glazunov himself, marching along in the next column, biting his lip. Serves you right, mate. Look where your painting got you.

On and on trudges Holy Russia, the living and the dead all together. Some are wearing bast shoes, some sneakers.

Here's Ivan the Terrible, leaning heavily on his bloody staff, scratching his bonce underneath the crown with his ringed fingers.

There's Emelyan Pugachev with Stenka Razin — two brave peasant leaders!

And there's Catherine the Great, the nymphomaniac empress.

Dostoyevsky and Leo Tolstoy pass by arm in arm, discussing non-resistance to evil.

Pyotr Stolypin strides along with determined step, an overcoat thrown over his shoulders.

He is followed by the Georgian Joseph, nicknamed Stalin.

A little way on there's a junior barrister, Vladimir Ulyanov, nicknamed Lenin, with his sisters Manyasha and Dunyasha and his wife Nadyusha.

There's Grigory Rasputin, sloshed as usual, his face as red as his shirt, marching along without a care in the world, bawling ditties:

> *"In an arsehole I shall live,*
> *Be as merry as can be!*
> *Put in windows, make a door,*
> *Make it warm and cosy!"*

Here comes Holy Russia! Make way!

From the brown sky above little bits of something unlike rain or snow started to fall. They appeared to wriggle as they fell, slimy and revolting like worms.

Tryapkin the detective put up the collar on his raincoat to stop the worms from slipping down his back.

"Well," he thought to himself. "Here I am in Moscow."

We're All Long Dead

Translated by John Dewey

You're never so completely lonely as when you're in a car at night, and it's raining. Straight away I had to admit that this thought was really too long for me. Mine are usually much shorter and simpler, so this one clearly belonged to someone else — just like the car I was now driving, in fact. Heavy raindrops were battering the windscreen and the wipers couldn't cope any more. I turned in to the side and switched off the engine and headlights. The lights on the dashboard went out as well.

Now I was in pitch darkness on this god-forsaken road at dead of night.

Leaning back in my seat, I lit a cigarette. The patter of raindrops on the roof was pleasantly soothing. Soon the rain stopped, and, stuffing my cigarette-end into the ashtray, I drove on.

I was on my way to see my father, who used to be a sea captain but was now just a crazy old guy who went about all year in an open raincoat and darned striped vest, wearing his sailor's cap at a jaunty angle, and with a huge pipe clenched between his yellow, nicotine-stained teeth — a very expensive pipe it was too, presented to him by an English admiral for some wartime exploits or other.

It was five years or so since I'd last seen him. Then, the week before, quite out of the blue, I received a telegram: "Come iimediately: there's a little surprise waiting for you."

And then, naturally, it was signed: "Cap'n". That was what he called himself.

So I'd set off, without even knowing why, to be honest. Certainly not because of the "little surprise". I suspected this to be just another example of Dad playing the fool.

Why had I done it, then? Why, indeed, had I borrowed a friend's car and driven flat out for two days instead of simply buying a train ticket and stretching out on a couchette, to wake up at my destination the following morning?

I don't know... I really don't... There are things which one can't explain logically and which you don't even want to explain.

It was nearly morning — about five o'clock, in fact — by the time I reached the town. I decided to book in at a hotel. A young girl with a fringe down to her eyes was sitting behind a glass screen in the empty lobby. Aware that I was looking at her, the girl raised her head from the book she was reading.

"The night train to Germany has already left," she said, smiling.

"Pardon me?" I asked, perplexed.

"That's what it says here, in the novel," the girl explained. "It's a beautiful sentence, don't you think?"

It was just a sentence. Nothing special.

"Sure," I said.

"D'you want to stay at this hotel?"

"Yes," I nodded. "Assuming that you have a vacant room, of course."

"You assume correctly," laughed the girl, holding out a blank form. I quickly filled it out.

There was a pause.

"Is the book interesting?" I asked, to make conversation.

"Well, there's this hero who wakes up one morning, has breakfast, and then he goes to work..."

"*What* an original plot!"

We laughed.

Sticking out a delightful little pink tongue, the girl flicked it rapidly over her full lips.

"Let's have a kiss, then," I coaxed, laying on the old charm.

"You are a fast one, and no mistake," she said. Clenching her fingers into fists she lifted them to shoulder-height and then stretched languorously.

"It's just that I'm in a sexy mood today," I said as if in justification.

"Ri-i-ight." There was an irresistibly playful lilt to her voice. "Well, come on then. But through the glass, mind."

"Kissing through glass," I declared in a dogmatic tone, "is like smelling flowers in a gas mask."

"Well, I suppose that could be quite nice too."

Taking the initiative, the girl held her face to the screen, and we kissed.

"Have you ever kissed a dead person on the lips?" she asked quite unexpectedly.

"I can see you're keen on horror stories," I chuckled.

"Ooh, no," the girl replied with a mock shudder. "I don't like horror stories."

"What about love stories?"

"Ooh, no," she said, continuing the game. "I get all excited."

"What about..."

"Quiet!" snapped the girl, jerking her forefinger in the air. "Can you hear the music?"

I listened, but couldn't hear any music.

After a minute she said, "Have you ever had the feeling that it's all stage scenery? These buildings, cars, people. Our whole life. Sometimes I even get the feeling that I simply don't exist, that I'm just a piece of scenery too."

"I don't know," I replied with a slight frown. "I've never thought about it."

Everything had started off so well, yet now here I was bogged down in this stupid conversation that was verging on the mystical.

"So what brings you here?" she changed the subject suddenly.

"I've come to visit my dad," I said. "He used to be a sea captain, you know."

"Oh, I know him!" exclaimed the girl, coming alive. "That strange old bloke who always went around in an open raincoat, summer and winter."

"That's right," I confirmed. "And a striped sailor's vest."

"I think he's dead," said the girl, frowning. "Yes, that's right. He's dead."

Dead?.. Dead?!.. How extraordinary!... Was this perhaps the "little surprise" I'd been promised in the telegram? Well, it would be quite in character...

"When did he die?" I enquired.

"A long time ago," she replied with a shrug. "It must be about a year now."

When? When?

"About a year ago... I know because a friend of mine lives in the same building."

Hmm... a year ago. Yet the telegram had been sent about ten days ago.

"Where's his grave, then?" I asked, stupidly.

The girl hooted with laughter.

"Where do you think — in the cemetery, naturally. Then there was that odd name he always used," she recalled. "Cap... Cap..."

"Cap'n," I said. "He called himself The Cap'n."

"Yes," the girl nodded. "That's it: The Cap'n. My name's Kira, by the way," she added, and smoothed her hair.

"Pleased to meet you," I said, taking my key and heading slowly up the stairs.

"Sleep tight," Kira called after me.

2.

I had a dream in the style of a '30s film: brisk, jolly music blaring from loudspeakers in the park; plump girls in white dresses strolling along the paths; smart officers in shining boots, also out for a stroll. As for me, I was sitting in a little boat in the middle of a pond with a panama hat on my head, holding a fishing rod. Not far away a natty little steamer with the name 'DEATH' on it was sailing past.

As this was a dream, both the steamer on the pond and its name seemed quite normal.

When I opened my eyes, for a second or so I thought I was still dreaming. A strange man in black was standing by the door. Black patent-leather shoes, impeccably pressed black trousers, a black overcoat (unbuttoned), a black jacket (buttoned)... A black hat, black gloves and a black walking-stick completed the overall picture.

"Mr Schulz," said the strange man by way of introduction, "Pyotr Ilyich. I'm an old friend of The Cap'n."

Kira burst into the room all out of breath and launched into an indignant tirade:

"Now listen, just what do you think you're up to? Walking in here as if you owned the place! Didn't you hear me call — are you hard of hearing, or what?!"

"Pyo-tr Il-yich," I repeated, as if savouring the name and patronymic on my tongue. "You don't happen to compose music, do you?"

"Bah! Music!" Kira scoffed contemptuously. "He happens to be an undertaker, that's what."

"No, I don't compose music," Mr Schulz replied in his somewhat toneless voice, completely ignoring Kira. "Actually, I'm the proprietor of a modest establishment known as Bon Voyage. Wreaths, coffins and ribbons at twenty per cent below state prices."

"I heard that my father has passed away: is that right?" I asked, pulling on my trousers.

"That would be putting it mildly," muttered Mr Schulz in an off-hand manner.

"But hang on — what about the telegram, then?"

"I sent you that."

"I don't get any of this," I said, my head spinning.

"Don't worry, I'll explain," promised Mr Schulz, adding with a sideways glance at Kira: "Only not here."

Outside in the street a fine drizzle was falling. Mr Schulz strode out at such a brisk pace that I could hardly keep up with him. Soon we arrived at the cemetery.

It was a cemetery like any other. Graves, headstones, a hushed silence... Mr Schulz, excusing himself, popped into a little house to the right of the cemetery gates, soon to re-appear holding a long iron bar.

"Come on," he said.

Following one of the paths, we walked further and further to the end of the cemetery. Here, next to a luxuriant bird-cherry bush, was my father's grave, with the following inscription emblazoned on its modest headstone:

"Even now I am more alive than the living... The Cap'n."

"He thought that up himself," said Mr Schulz (whether as a disclaimer of responsibility or a simple statement of fact was not quite clear).

Then, handing me the iron bar, he commanded: "Stick it in." I stuck it in. Practically the whole length of the bar disappeared into soft earth.

"So what?" I said, turning to Mr Schulz. And in the same split second I realized what.

There was no coffin.

Mr Schulz made no response but headed for the way out.

We entered a cafe not far from the cemetery. Here we bought a small coffee each and found somewhere to sit in an out-of-the-way corner.

"When I was about four months old," declared Mr Schulz, taking a sip from his cup, "my father threw me up high in the air..." He bit off a piece of biscuit and chewed thoughtfully. "But he didn't manage to catch me."

"Yes," I said, "accidents can happen."

From an inside pocket of his overcoat he swiftly pulled out a thick wad of photographs held together with a rubber band, and threw them on the table. He looked at me expectantly.

I drew them towards me cautiously, with a vague premonition of something very nasty. I was not mistaken. They were all, without exception, pictures of funerals. Or more exactly, not actual funerals, but the faces of the dead in their coffins. In close-up.

There were all sorts of people — old men, children, young women, young men, teenagers... I slowly examined each picture in turn before laying it aside. I can't say this gave me any great aesthetic pleasure.

"Your father took the pictures," explained Mr Schulz. "There are about a hundred here."

"Actually, I don't quite..." I faltered... and then I cut myself short as in the cemetery not long before.

Sorting through the photographs, I suddenly saw one of Kira. It was in colour, and I recognized her light-blue dress, the one she had been wearing at the hotel reception desk. It was Kira, without a doubt — only not alive, but dead. Her eyes were shut, her hair was neatly combed, and her hands lay lifeless on her breast; a thin candle had been inserted between the fingers.

I shot a questioning glance at Mr Schulz.

"Those marked on the back with a small red cross," he declared in a subdued tone, "*have returned.*"

What did he mean by that? Hastily I turned over Kira's photograph. A thick red cross had been drawn in the bottom right-hand corner...

I recalled what she had said: "Sometimes I get the feeling that I simply don't exist." Now these words took on a completely different meaning.

Outside a car drove past. Somewhere in the distance a dog barked. There was a roaring sound in my ears. I opened my mouth wide and then closed it again. Sometimes this helps, but it didn't now. A young girl came into the cafe, went to the juke box, inserted a coin and began quietly swaying her head in time to the song that started playing.

"Sometimes I get the feeling that I simply don't exist," I repeated out loud.

"What?" asked Mr Schulz, not catching what I had said.

"Nothing," I replied, and emptied my coffee-cup. "Carry on."

"What more is there to say?" he said, looking at me with a puzzled air. "The dead return. On that occasion..."

"Just a moment," I interrupted, and went to the counter. "Do you have any vodka?" I asked the tall woman who was serving.

"Vodka?" Her pencilled eyebrows shot up. "This happens to be a children's cafe, in case you didn't know."

But on taking a second look at my face, she disappeared behind a curtain without further comment. A minute later she re-appeared with a cut-glass tumbler. I downed it and returned to my seat.

"On that occasion..." I said.

"What?" asked Mr Schulz.

"You said: 'On that occasion'."

"Ah," he remembered. "On that occasion The Cap'n took a cylinder of compressed air and got into his coffin. Then my assistant and I buried him at the cemetery. Next day the coffin had disappeared. That's all there is to it."

"Could somebody have dug him up without being detected?"

Mr Schulz heaved a noisy sigh.

"No," he said firmly. "We sat next to the grave all night. It poured with rain, too. We got soaked through."

A bevy of schoolgirls crowded into the cafe. Giggling and chattering, they began eating scoops of ice cream of various colours. My head had started to ache — or rather, my temples. Gradually the vodka was having an effect on me; already I was beginning to think that our visit to the cemetery and the conversation we were now having were all a hoax. A common-or-garden hoax.

But Mr Schulz was sombre as he sat there opposite me.

"Why did you send for me?" I asked straight out.

He chewed his lips.

"I thought you'd want to know all this."

"Oh, I do," I said sarcastically, nodding my head. "I do indeed."

"Apart from which," continued Mr Schulz, twisting his empty cup in his hands, "I thought perhaps you'd have a go as well. After all, he was your father. That's about the long and the short of it..."

Aha, so that was it... I massaged my temples, which felt as if they were splitting.

"Forget it..."

"Well anyway," he declared emphatically, rising to his feet, "I'll see to the grave, and get your coffin and air cylinders ready. You just think about it very carefully."

Mr Schulz gave a slight bow and left the cafe, while I remained seated at the table, staring vacantly and fixedly in one direction. My head felt empty...

3.

The following day I took Kira to the cinema. Gunshots rang out from the screen. We were sitting in the back row, and I was pulling segments off a tangerine and putting them in Kira's mouth; sometimes her lips brushed the tips of my fingers. As the story unfolded, the film stars started making love, and leaning towards me, she whispered in my ear:

"I'd like to have a baby. A little girl."

"I can help you with this. I seem to father only girls." I whispered into her ear.

She scoffed in answer and the film ended. We went outside. It was very warm, more like a summer than a spring evening. Television screens glimmered in windows.

"Why did you kiss me then?" asked Kira.

"When?" I queried, momentarily at a loss.

"In the hotel. Through the glass."

"Ah," I smiled. "Who'd miss out on kissing a pretty face?"

She pouted provocatively.

"I don't like people saying I'm pretty."

"In that case," I suggested, "let me kiss you again."

"I've never yet given anyone a real kiss," Kira declared indignantly. "Believe me, I'm not interested in *that*."

"What are you interested in, then?"

Instead of answering she looked up at the sky.

"You see that red ring round the moon?" she said, pointing. "It's a bad omen. There'll be trouble before the year is through."

I too looked up at the moon, but I couldn't see a ring.

"Trouble before this year is through," I declaimed. "Either I shall die, or you."

"He-ey," she intoned admiringly, "you're a poet!"

"Indeed I am," I conceded.

"Do you know this poem, then?" She stopped and began to recite:

Once somebody walked past beneath my window.
I think that it was raining; I think there was thunder, too.
Once somebody said 'farewell' to me.
I think it was on the veranda; I think we were having tea.
Once somebody left me, never to return.
I think it was a Tuesday — or Wednesday, who can say?"

"No," I said, "I don't know that one. Who's it by?"

"Me," replied Kira.

We turned off into a side street and then another... Slowly we strolled through unlit, narrow streets. Even the occasional passers-by had disappeared by now.

All at once, without warning, Kira gave voice to a full-throated "A-a-ah!" and smiled with delight. "How lovely! There's nobody here. I like the night-time." She thrust her hands into her trouser pockets and mischievously kicked an empty beer can.

"I like toys, too. Why don't they sell those toy snakes any more — you know the ones..." And taking her hand out of her pocket, she made writhing motions with her wrist. "They used to move like this. Why?" she demanded, almost petulantly. "You must remember them, those lovely green snakes."

"Yes, I remember," I said, although in fact I didn't.

"So why don't they sell them any more?" she asked, pouting her lips like a child.

"Because your childhood is over," I replied brutally.

Immediately Kira seemed to wilt, and she said no more.

The sky was veiled with clouds now. A sharp wind got up and it began to drizzle.

Ahead of us we saw the cemetery.

The neon sign "Bon Voyage!" was flickering over the entrance to the funeral parlour.

Mr Schulz was not in the least surprised that we should visit him so late. He and a muscle-bound hulk of a fellow were seated at a table, playing cards.

On the floor, not far from the front door, stood a spacious coffin.

"Pyotr Ilyich," I asked, "can we wait here until the rain stops?"

"You can do what you like here, as long as you pay," joked Mr Schulz. He was in a good mood. "Would you like a game of cards?"

I declined.

"A pity," he commented, and yawned expansively. "This is Alik," he added, with a casual nod in the direction of the hulk. "My assistant. I take it you haven't met?"

"How do you do, Alik," said Kira.

"You're wasting your time," pointed out Mr Schulz. "He's deaf and dumb. Would you like some hot milk?"

"I would," Kira replied.

Mr Schulz went to the kitchen and returned with a large cup of hot milk.

"There you are, young lady," he said, offering the cup to Kira.

Kira kicked off her boots, curled up in a deep armchair and, cupping the milk with both hands, began to sip at leisure.

"Excuse my asking, Pyotr Ilyich," she said, "but do you happen to know where I might find the grave of a young man who was killed in a motor-cycle accident two years ago?"

"As it happens, I do. But why do you want to know?"

"He was my first love," explained Kira, blushing.

"First love — that's a good one," said Mr Schulz and began shuffling the cards. "You don't even know where his grave is."

"People don't always regret the loss of their loved ones," Kira said quietly.

I left to wander round the parlour, examining the coffins. There were all sorts, even one with all the modern conveniences.

When I returned, I found a lively conversation in progress. Mr Schulz was relating something with great enthusiasm. Kira was laughing out loud: there was no sign of the melancholy mood she had been in before. Her cheeks were flushed, her eyes sparkled as if she were drinking spirits rather than milk.

"Why don't you get married, Pyotr Ilyich?" Kira asked playfully.

"Because all women are potential whores!" came his answer as quick as a flash.

"Wha-at?!" spluttered Kira in mock indignation. "So according to you, I'm a whore too?!"

"Of course!" declared Mr Schulz confidently.

"What a knave you are!" chortled Kira, leaning back in the motley-patterned armchair.

"Yes, a knave of hearts," confirmed Mr Schulz in an impish tone, rolling up his eyes to reveal the whites, and sticking his long tongue out to one side.

"What a performer!" cried Kira with delight, clapping her hands.

Alik the deaf-mute impatiently rapped his knuckles on the cards scattered on the table, but Mr Schulz had lost his enthusiasm for the game.

"Indeed I am a performer," he concurred readily. "Before finding my true vocation here at the cemetery, I spent many years working in a circus. As a magician, actually."

"Oh, so you're a magician," said Kira, her eyes narrowing vindictively. "We'll put that to the test straight away. Right, then: tell us what we were talking about just before we got here."

She wiggled her shoulders with excitement.

Mr Schulz's face took on an intense, solemn expression.

"You were reciting poetry," he proclaimed in a sepulchral voice. "Am I right?"

"Got it in one!" shouted Kira, jumping up and down. "Long live, Mr Magician!"

"Do you like poetry, Pyotr Ilyich?" I asked.

"I do, rather," he nodded. "Best of all I like that poet... What's his name?.. Anyway, it doesn't matter. There's one poem by him. My all-time favourite... Hang on, how does it go? Ah, yes:

> *Ti — tum — ti — tum*
> *It's night!*
> *Ti — tum — ti — tum*
> *Take flight!*

"What a *splendid* poem!" laughed Kira, tossing her head back and shaking her thick hair. "So, what else did we talk about, Mr Magician?"

"What else?" Mr Schulz furrowed his brow. "Apart from that, you were talking about people's different aims in life."

"Wrong, you've got it wrong!" shouted Kira. "Nowhere near — nowhere near!"

"Well, all right, you didn't exactly discuss that, but in general... you philosophized."

"That's true, in principle," I confirmed.

"So what about you, Pyotr Ilyich: what would you like to be?" Kira asked.

"A fly," replied Mr Schulz without pausing for thought.

"How do you mean?" Kira actually straightened up slightly with surprise.

"Just what I said: a fly," declared Mr Schulz, vigorously describing circles in the air with his forefinger. "What's wrong with that? It would be great: flying round the room to your heart's content, and buzzing."

The deaf-mute gathered the cards into a pack and stalked out, the picture of injured pride.

"Bzzzzzz," buzzed Mr Schulz, scampering round the room.

This time Kira was even more convulsed with laughter.

"If you're a magician," she said when she had recovered, "do some magic."

"No problem," rejoined Mr Schulz. There was a brazen note in his voice. "But you'll have to help me, Kira my sweet."

"All right," agreed Kira eagerly, rising to her feet. "What do I have to do, then?"

Somehow all this was beginning to jar on me... In particular, I didn't like the intense look in Mr Schulz's beady little eyes.

"It's getting late, Kira," I said, grasping her arm. "We have to go."

"No way," she retorted, pulling herself free. "I'm not going until I've seen some magic."

Mr Schulz whistled: "Fyootee-fyoot", and, flicking his cane up to the ceiling, said, "My cane will turn into a sword."

And indeed, he now held in his hands a long thin blade.

"Is that all there is to your trick?" Kira asked, disappointed. "Pooh! And I was thinking..."

She had already turned to leave.

"Stop, stop!" called Mr Schulz cheerfully, holding her back.

"The main trick is still to come. Look into my eyes and pay attention. Now for some hocus-pocus... One! Two!! Three!!! Allez-oop!"

With these words Mr Schulz brandished the sharp blade and... cut off Kira's head!

At first I simply couldn't understand. My conscious mind just refused to accept as real what had taken place before my very eyes. It had been so grotesque... so sudden... so wild... The blade, entering Kira's neck, had sliced through it easily and without resistance. Her head had fallen to the floor.

"Eh?.. Eh?.." was all I could get out.

" 'ay is for 'orses," said Mr Schulz calmly. "Close your mouth, or you'll catch a fly."

The body had not slumped to the floor with a dull thud; no dark blood had come gushing out all over the furniture and walls... Nothing even remotely like this had happened... The head had rolled under the table, and now lay there. As for Kira's decapitated body, it just carried on standing in the same place as before.

"A graft," said Mr Schulz tersely.

"What?" I asked in a state of shock.

"I call them 'grafts'," he explained. "Those who have returned, that is. Why, didn't you realize from our conversation yesterday that they aren't human any more?"

My legs gave way. I sat down.

"No," I mumbled, "to tell the truth..." — but I was too dazed to continue.

Mr Schulz evidently sensed the state I was in.

"Go and sleep now," he advised. "Alik has made up a bed for you."

I nodded apathetically, and slowly, on legs like jelly, went up to... to Kira and took a look in through her neck.

It was empty and dark in there.

4.

When I entered the room next day, having slept until nearly midday, I came across a familiar scene. Mr Schulz and his deaf-

and-dumb assistant were playing cards. Kira was sitting in an armchair — minus her head, of course.

"You might at least have put her out of the way somewhere," I said with a sidelong glance at the body.

"What for?" asked Mr Schulz, genuinely surprised. "Let her sit there. She doesn't bother us for food or drink. There's even a peculiar kind of aesthetic appeal to it. The aesthetics of putrefaction." He quickly shuffled the cards. "Will you have a game?"

"No, thanks," I said.

"A pity," commented Mr Schulz, and yawned. "Then try out your coffin."

He was in no doubt whatsoever as to what my decision would be. He knew.

I got into the coffin, lay down and fixed my eyes on the ceiling. There was a cheap-looking chandelier up there, with some flies buzzing around it. I began to feel good inside. At peace.

"It's my belief," I said, "that everyone should spend at least an hour a day lying in their coffin, meditating about the point of their existence. It's so spiritually purifying."

Mr Schulz brought two large cylinders from the next room.

"Here you are," he said, placing them next to me. "Compressed air. You can purify yourself to your heart's content."

Towards midnight we dragged the coffin to the grave, which had been dug earlier. With well-practised movements Alik took a hammer and nails out of his bag.

"Listen!" I protested on seeing the deaf-mute's preparations. "What are you up to — you're not going to nail the lid down, are you?"

"For a start, you can stop yelling and getting worked up about nothing. And anyway, everything's got to be done for real. Otherwise what's the point?"

I heaved a sigh and climbed into the coffin without a word. It felt uncomfortable lying there. The cylinders were sticking into my sides quite painfully... At last I managed to settle myself more or less. Above me hung the black sky. No moon to be seen, no stars. Nothing but darkness...

My heart sank.

"Lord," I thought, "how dismal it is indeed to die in early spring."

"My, you're a poet," sniggered Mr Schulz, and gestured to Alik to nail down the coffin.

"You might as well dispense with the formal goodbyes, Pyotr Ilyich," I said sarcastically.

Mr Schulz rummaged in the pocket of his black overcoat.

"Here, take this," he said, holding out a grimy-looking sweet. "It's chocolate."

On the stroke of midnight they shovelled earth over me. When I started to have difficulty breathing, I took the rubber tube in my mouth and opened the valve in one of the cylinders.

So there I was, lying in a coffin, in the cemetery, under a thick layer of earth.

Buried...

Soon afterwards I heard a sort of scratching sound from above, as if somebody had scraped the lid of the coffin with something sharp.

I blinked...

It must have been in that instant, while I was blinking, that it all happened.

I was lying in a forest. The coffin had gone. It was a sunny day, and the birds were singing.

I stood up, dusted off my trousers and started walking.

I wandered slowly through the green grass, kicking at the yellow heads of flowers in my path... And suddenly I was overcome by a quite unexpected feeling of joy. It just hit me like an avalanche.

I was alive!

I could have died! I was supposed to die! But I was alive! Here I was, walking through a birch forest, kicking yellow flower heads, and there was an orange sun in the sky — the rising sun! For already it was dawn, and dawn would soon be followed by day. A new day!

The plethora of emotions surging through me made me want to shout out loud.

And so I did: "Hurray!"

"Who are you, some kind of nut?"

Not far off stood a middle-aged man in a jersey. To judge by his appearance, he was a typical holidaymaker staying at some nearby dacha.

"Yes, I'm a nut," I gladly conceded. "But tell me, how can I get into town?"

"That's the railway halt just over there," he pointed out.

There was indeed a platform, and a suburban train was already approaching, sounding its thin, quavering hooter. I broke into a run and just managed to scramble into the last carriage.

I leaned back on the hard seat and looked out of the window. I felt... I felt... No, I didn't feel anything. I just looked out of the window, rejoicing at the sight of everything gliding past the dirty pane of glass.

Before going to Mr Schulz I walked around for a bit. I went to the cinema and had a look at an exhibition of children's drawings...

I found everything interesting: it all gave me the most intense pleasure... For a long time I stood in front of the window of a women's clothes shop, examining the dummies. I was immediately reminded of Kira, of us kissing through the glass — and then of Mr Schulz cutting her head off. A light drizzle had started up again and I went into a public toilet. A pigeon was sitting on the window-sill, its feathers ruffled. There was a one-ruble note lying in the lavatory pan. I pissed on it and left, setting off for the cemetery.

There was an Orthodox cross on my grave, and two wilting carnations lay on the mound of earth.

Mr Schulz was having breakfast. Thinly cut slices of cheese and smoked sausage were laid out on little plates. Kira was still sitting in the armchair as before.

"He-llo, squire," he called out cheerfully on seeing me. "Welcome back!"

"Thank you," I replied, and poured myself some coffee from the pot. "Listen, Mr Schulz, who put those stupid flowers on my grave?"

"I did," said Mr Schulz. "In your memory."

"Why, were you so sure I wasn't coming back?"

"Of course. It's been a whole year."

I nearly choked on my coffee...

"How could a whole year have passed?"

"Quite simply," replied Mr Schulz, busily spreading a large piece of butter on a large piece of white bread.

"We-ell..." I said.

What else could I say in the circumstances?

"We-ell..." Mr Schulz repeated after me, and added: "Go on, tell me what happened."

I told him... Although basically there was nothing to tell.

We sat in silence, Mr Schulz picked his teeth.

"We-ell," he drawled again. "So we have an interesting scenario here. Assuming that about fifty million people die every year, and someone is bringing them back to life again, what do we conclude? That we're all long dead."

"I don't suppose they bring *everybody* back to life," I mused. "All in all we're left with a whole lot of unanswered questions. Er, for example..." But no example sprang immediately to mind, since it was *all* just one big unanswered question. "Er, for example..." I repeated, "what about identity papers, or the whole question of property and living space? And then, what if people bump into their former relatives? There could be all sorts of problems. Anyway, what's it all for? What's the point?"

I lit a cigarette and inhaled avidly.

"My dear fellow," replied Mr Schulz in a condescending tone, "when bees have all their honey taken away from them without so much as a by-your-leave, I think they're left with a lot of unanswered questions too. After all, they gathered the honey, intending to feed their little ones. And suddenly: gone, the whole lot of it — every last drop! So don't worry your head on that score. I think it all makes sense to them. As for our 'unanswered questions', they couldn't care less about them."

"Well... I don't know."

"There is nothing to know," he rejoined, standing up and stretching himself lazily. " 'There are more things in heaven and earth, Horatio, than are dreamt of in your philosophy!' " And turning his face towards me, enunciating clearly, he said: "Ey-jiz..."

I looked at him perplexed.

"*Ey-jiz.* That's English for 'eternity'."

"What about it?" I asked, not getting his drift.

"Nothing," said Mr Schulz. "It's just that I bumped into The Cap'n in town yesterday."

5.

We didn't have to wait long for Dad to show up: he appeared the following day towards evening. As always, he was wearing his unbuttoned raincoat, striped vest and sailor's cap — and, of course, he had that pipe clenched between his teeth.

"Ahoy, shipmates," he said in a breezy tone, as if he hadn't disappeared for two years but simply gone out for a walk for an hour or so. "How's tricks, sonny boy?" he asked with a wink in my direction.

"All right, Dad," I replied.

"Pah! Dad!" scowled Mr Schulz. "He's no more your father than I'm Tchaikovsky."

The Captain gingerly touched the glistening flank of the teapot.

"Right then, me hearties," he proposed, "shall we knock back some tea?"

"Listen, mate," hissed Mr Schulz, breathing heavily. "Cut out the play-acting."

Dad's bushy eyebrows shot up.

"Pyotr, old shipmate," he said, "I don't know what you're talking about."

"Ha, just give it a rest," rasped Mr Schulz with even more of a scowl. "You understand everything perfectly!"

"Ve-ery well!" said Dad, striking the table with the palm of his hand to emphasize his words. "Let's put our cards on the table. Secret project 'X'. Re-cycling of waste material. Ultimate goal: the conquest of other planets... After all, what's the point of letting assets rot away in the ground?" he said, breaking into a strident laugh, and I flinched involuntarily. How well I knew that staccato laugh.

"Is it the re-cycling of corpses we're talking about here?" enquired Mr Schulz with feigned innocence. "As cosmonauts, yes?"

"The outer shell," my father corrected him gently. "Just the outer shell. The rest is discarded as surplus to requirements. So..."

"You can stop spinning us a yarn," Mr Schulz interrupted in an icy tone, and then continued, prodding my father with his finger: "He — I don't mean you, but the one this body really belonged to — he rumbled *you* straight away. And that's why you killed him. Well, isn't that how it was?"

"No," said my father. "Or rather," he continued after a brief pause, "maybe it was, and maybe..."

"Oh yes, oh yes," Mr Schulz promptly cut in.

"What are you getting at, Mr Schulz, or whatever it is you call yourself?"

A distinct quiver of hatred had entered my father's voice.

"Don't pretend you don't know," retorted Schulz, leaping abruptly from his seat.

"There's something fishy about all this," I thought, looking from my father to Mr Schulz and back again. "Something definitely..."

However, I didn't manage to complete my train of thought. Mr Schulz suddenly started waving his arms and gabbling nineteen to the dozen in a shrill-sounding language like the twittering of birds. My father started chirping like a bird as well. Mr Schulz lurched towards the table, where his cane was lying. From his appearance he was clearly in a resolute frame of mind, to say the very least... When he grasped the cane, I realized exactly what was going to happen.

"Hand over that cane!" my father commanded, holding out his hand. "And don't try any funny stuff, right?"

Mr Schulz froze on the spot. His face was twisted with malice.

"Here!" he shouted in a hoarse voice, and with a flourish threw the cane at my father's feet.

Dad bent down with a triumphant smirk... In that split second Mr Schulz whipped a shiny little box out of his pocket and aimed it at the stooping captain. There was a soft (I would even say velvety) buzzing sound.

Dad suddenly *burst* into flame, as if he'd been doused with petrol.

He straightened up, engulfed in flame, dropped the cane, took a few steps towards Mr Schulz, tottered... All this took place in absolute silence. I said nothing. Mr Schulz said nothing. My father said nothing... Then he began to collapse in upon himself. First his head sank through his shoulders and disappeared inside his trunk, then his legs disintegrated; and finally his body fell to the floor without a sound and also disintegrated...

All that remained of The Cap'n, my father, was an amorphous pile of ash.

Mr Schulz put the shiny gadget back in his pocket, fetched a dustpan and brush, painstakingly swept everything into a pile and then into the dustpan and, half-opening the window, emptied the ash outside.

"There's our life for you," he proclaimed gloomily, and began to rummage for something in a cupboard. "We are all ash in the wind. Am I right in thinking there's a novel of that title, by a German writer?"

"Yes, there is," I confirmed. "Except it's called 'We Are Not Dust in the Wind'."

"Well, it's not important," said Mr Schulz with a dismissive wave of the hand, and produced Kira's head from the cupboard.

He placed the head on her shoulders and started quickly applying something like cement or plasticine to her neck, rubbing it in. At least, that's what it looked like from where I was standing.

"That's it!" announced Mr Schulz after five minutes.

I had been watching Kira continuously. She opened her eyes and looked around with an air of slight bewilderment.

"Excuse me," she said, "I seem to have dozed off."

"Don't worry about it," rejoined Mr Schulz, giving me a conspiratorial wink.

"Oh!" cried Kira, looking at her watch and jumping up. "I'm on duty at half past seven. Well, I must dash. See you tomorrow, love." And she was off.

"So you too," I said slowly. "You too... But I don't understand... why you had to pull the wool over my eyes... why you had to bury me in the cemetery..."

"And I don't understand your passion for logical-empirical systems," declared Mr Schulz as he poured strong tea into two cups. "If you put two and two together, why do you necessarily have to end up with four? Why not twenty-two? Eh?"

"... is for 'orses," I said, pulling the sugar bowl towards me and putting two spoonfuls of sugar in my cup. "Don't give me all this flannel. I just want a straight answer: are you an alien?!"

"Good Lord!" exclaimed Mr Schulz, holding his head in his hands in mock dismay. "You know, I really think you've flipped. You're quite obsessed with these aliens." He suddenly broke into a loud guffaw. "Just the slightest provocation, and out you come with your flying saucers, cosmic forces, other worlds... I don't understand," he said, shaking his head.

"And there's something else I don't understand..." I tried to say.

"Ah, but I know exactly what you're going to say now," Mr Schulz interrupted me with a sour expression. "Only don't think I'm going to explain anything to you, because I'm not. You wouldn't understand a thing, anyway."

"Perhaps I would," I said, not giving up. "Give me a try."

"Your mother did that when she had you... No, joking apart, there's no point. It would be as if I were to switch into ancient Persian now, in the middle of a sentence. What would you understand then?"

"There's only one thing I do understand," I said stubbornly. "That they are extra-terrestrials" (I nodded in the direction of the window to indicate my father's scattered remains), "and that you are too. So tell me, not in ancient Persian but in plain Russian: *why are you here?* What the hell do you want here? And why are you reanimating our corpses?"

"Phe-ew," puffed Mr Schulz. "Quite honestly, your head's filled with a kind of verbal mish-mash, young man. And not just you personally" (shaping a sphere in the air with his hands), "but all of you here on the planet Earth. What a load of rubbish you've stuffed your heads with! Extra-terrestrials, outer space... Well, none of this exists. There is no outer space. *It doesn't exist.*"

"What do you mean?" I must admit this was the last thing I'd expected to hear. "But what about the stars? And the other planets?"

"There aren't any other planets," Mr Schulz explained patiently. "There isn't *anything* at all. So there's no need to get in a stew and make life complicated for yourselves. What a way of going on, really! There's a nice proverb you have here, a French one: 'It's not true that life is simple: it's much simpler'."

"I don't understand anything," I mumbled. "I don't understand a damned thing."

"I did warn you that you wouldn't understand," Mr Schulz lectured me. "Console yourself with the thought that you have succeeded in fulfilling your purpose here on earth. That's something not everyone manages, quite frankly."

"Hang on, hang on," I appealed in sudden animation. "So just what is my purpose here on earth?"

"To come here, of course. To have these conversations with me."

"And is that all?" I asked, dumbfounded.

"That's all," nodded Mr Schulz. "Why, did you have visions of something universal again?"

A breeze blew in through the half-open window making the blind flap. "What a strange thing life is, though," I thought.

"What a strange thing life is, though!" I said out loud. "There's you and me sitting here, talking. Outside it's spring. Some people are lying buried in the cemetery; others, as yet still alive, are suffering, rejoicing, lamenting, falling in love, sleeping, eating..."

"Get to the point," Mr Schulz interrupted impatiently. "Stop waffling. What is it you want to say?"

"Or take you, for instance," I continued, ignoring his remark. "Who are you? Where are you from? And then, this whole weird business..."

"You talk too much," he remarked again.

"No, you see..." I went on, not listening — but immediately brought myself up short. "The universe doesn't exist... That's beyond belief..."

Mr Schulz sniggered, rubbing his hands with satisfaction.

"You can't believe it? I knew all along that you wouldn't."

"And we don't exist either?" I asked.

"That's right," he confirmed.

"Well, that's it," I thought. "Here we are. End of the line..."

"You know what," Mr Schulz said, "why don't you go back where you came from? I did give you a friendly warning that you wouldn't understand anything. Everything has its limitations, particularly the human intellect. So don't attempt to understand — or even less, explain — anything on the basis of your own thoughts and feelings. To put it crudely, quite by chance you've blundered into a maze with no way out again. A maze designed with no way out. You can understand that, I hope?"

"Well, more or less," I replied weakly.

Suddenly I felt dead tired and drained of all mental energy.

"So go back again, seeing that you're so tired," Mr Schulz urged me. "After all, you have a female, don't you, or whatever it is you call them here — a girlfriend?"

I remembered Masha, a peroxide blonde in black silk stockings.

"Yes," I nodded, "I have a female."

"Well, off you go, then," he said, giving me a friendly pat on the shoulder.

And I did...

To be more precise, first of all I went out into the street. As I recall, it still hadn't stopped raining. I walked past my grave, where I'd been buried a year before, and leaving the cemetery wandered round my native town, past everything that had once gone to make up my childhood, adolescence and youth. And which, according to Mr Schulz, simply didn't exist.

Then I came to the station, where I purchased a ticket and boarded my train. For some reason the lights in the carriage weren't switched on, and we sped through the endless expanses of Russia in pitch darkness. More than half the seats in the carriage were occupied by deaf-mutes who were inarticulately mumbling among themselves. A musician was telling no-one in particular how he had had his violin and all his money stolen. He was on the top bunk, travelling on a warrant issued by the police. Opposite me sat a stout woman who spent half the night reminiscing about how as a young girl she'd seen a UFO over the pigsty in her village. There wasn't enough bed linen for everyone. I spread a mattress on one of the middle bunks and, stuffing my rather new shoes under the rather grubby pillow, fell into a deep sleep.

When I woke up, the train had already stopped and there was nobody in the carriage apart from myself. I made for the way out. On the platform I saw the train attendant.

"Goodbye, then," I said to her.

"Blow me!" she chortled. "And I thought you were deaf and dumb too."

Passing through the station building, I came out into the town. In a restaurant I found Masha: it was where I had left her a year before. She was sitting with her legs crossed, sipping a milkshake through a straw.

"Oh, it's you," she said without enthusiasm.

"Yes," I said, "it's me."

Actually, I wasn't completely convinced of this.

I took a cigarette from its packet and put it between my lips without lighting it.

"We're all dead," I said, and the cigarette jumped up and down in time with my words. "We all died a long time ago."

"You seem a bit touchy or something today," commented Masha and, leaning slightly towards me over the table, patted me on the cheek like a dog. "What's up, sweetie?" she asked with a faint, languid laugh. "Knotty problems? Well, don't lose any sleep over them. You know what the French say: 'It's not true that life is simple: it is much simpler'."

With these words Masha swiftly pulled a shiny little box out of her handbag and held it right in front of my face.

My heart missed a beat. However, it was only a cigarette lighter.

The Autumn Carnival of Death

Translated by José Alaniz

One Autumn evening I was sitting at home, writing a story about love. Simply about love. About love and nothing but.

A young man meets a girl. Through the narrow alleys of some little seaside town, they reach the sea and plod along the beach...

Deserted. Dusky. Empty of people.

Because it's already November. Winter. And summer's not coming anytime soon.

In other words, crap.

But I liked it. Even though I didn't know how to end the story. So I set the story aside and switched on the television. The host of some talk show was interviewing people who had experienced clinical death.

"We were at a birthday party," a girl was saying, in a troubled voice. "Then we decided to have a swim..."

"This was a lake, right?" asked the host.

"Right, a lake. And, kidding around, they pushed me into the water. Suddenly I found myself in pitch darkness." The girl fell silent. "And then I saw a bright, shining light... A woman came out of the light and said, 'Hello. My name is Elizabeth.' She took me by the hand and led me to Heaven."

"Heaven? That's what you think now?"

"No, that's what I felt then, that it was Heaven. All around there was this bright light and out of this light there came this sensation of love, joy, contentment. I was simply surrounded by love, it was literally pulsating."

"And who was this Elizabeth?" asked the host.

"My guardian angel... guardian angel..." the girl repeated, twice. "That's what I think. Overall, dying is cool!"

"But you came back, didn't you?"

"Yeah, I came back. Because Elizabeth said it wasn't my time yet. And I said, 'But I don't know how to go back.' And Elizabeth said, 'See you...' And I woke up in the hospital."

A heavy-set Black woman got up from her chair.

"I don't believe you can die and come back," she said, talking very fast. "I think death is death! You don't come back from it."

I turned off the television and, sitting down at my desk, wrote an ending to my story.

The heroine turns out to have an extremely rare disease, as a result of which, once a year, most often in the Spring, she falls into a faint without warning. The fainting spell can come at the most inappropriate time and in the most inappropriate place. It so happens that the heroine visits a swimming pool. And as she's climbing down the little ladder into the water, she has a fainting spell...

The story ended like this:

"There were many people in the swimming pool, but no one noticed how she drowned."

After typing the last period, I decided to go out for the mail. There were two letters in the box. One was from the library. It said my books were already three years overdue. Out of the second envelope, a postcard fell.

On the postcard was a picture of a beautiful, old-fashioned mansion with tall columns, and a park stretched out all around it. A very nice postcard. The text was also very nice, written in an obviously feminine hand:

"You are invited to our Autumn Carnival.

D."

And that was it.

No time, no place... Curious...

With this strange epistle in hand, I set off to visit my old friend, Mr. Schulz.

Mr. Schulz was drinking tea.

I handed him the postcard, "Have a look at this mysterious invitation. Perhaps you can guess the riddle? You have such a large store of life experience to draw upon."

"Yes, I've got life experience, alright," confirmed Mr. Schulz. "Well, let's see... let's see..."

Having turned the postcard over this way and that, he said:

"There's no mystery. 'D' is Death. She's inviting you to an Autumn carnival. You do like Autumn?"

"Sure. I like it."

"Well, there you are. Those who like Autumn, as a rule, die in Autumn."

I grew alarmed.

"But, Mr. Schulz..."

"Come, come, my boy... Now do you really think you'll live forever?"

"Not forever, but..."

"Oh, do drop it, now," he interrupted. "It would make some sense if we never died at all. But as things stand: a bit more, a bit less... What's the difference?"

Mr. Schulz resumed sipping his tea.

"Easy for you to philosophize," I retorted, in offense. "But what if..."

He interrupted again:

"Hey, you know what? Why don't you take your camera with you and ask Death if you can take her picture. Then you can blind her with the flash, and take off!"

"God, what nonsense!" I exclaimed angrily and left Mr. Schulz.

I came back home and turned on the radio.

"In love, we have to come to each other's aid," sang some French songbird, "for only then can we withstand this world. Come to my aid..."

The street lamps came on outside. Passersby gradually diminished in number and disappeared.

Night fell.

An old, black automobile appeared on the street. It moved very slowly. Driving up to the entrance of my building the car stopped.

I immediately understood this was meant for me, and stepped out.

The car doors opened. I slipped inside. The car set off. Again it moved very, very slowly.

There was no one inside the car. Not even a driver. The steering wheel turned by itself. Out the windows, some unfamiliar little streets swam by.

I dozed off to the hum of the engine.

When I woke up, the car had stopped in front of a beautiful home with tall columns. The same one as on the postcard.

The doors, decorated with fancy carvings, opened to reveal a wide marble staircase. On a soft carpet covering the steps, I climbed up to a brightly illuminated hall. An orchestra sat on a balcony. The conductor's white-gloved hands flew up — and there sounded a bewitching, unearthly melody.

I knew my classical music pretty well, but these eerie notes were completely alien to me.

Dancing couples began to whirl, rushing by in a vortex. And who wasn't there: harlequins in red and white tights, gnomes in caps with bells, elves with delicate dragonfly wings, princesses in crinolines, knights, clowns, mermaids. The bright colorful costumes dazzled my eyes.

A girl, in a white lace dress and golden mask, covering the upper portion of her face, rushed up to me.

"Are you bored?" she asked, looking into my eyes inquisitively. "Are you feeling down at our merry celebration?"

"No, no, of course not!" I wanted to reassure my new acquaintance. "It's just that, for me, all this is very unusual. This magic music, happy people, a beautiful hall... You have to understand that where I come from, there's nothing like this. Well, there is, but..."

"Let's not talk about anything sad," the girl smiled. "Let's dance. Listen, the melody's coming to an end. In a moment there'll be another."

Her fingers rested on my shoulders. And we glided smoothly over the black-and-white checkerboard floor.

"Take your mask off," I whispered in her ear. "Please..."

"I will, if you promise not to fall in love with me."

"I promise."

The girl fulfilled my request. And I saw her eyes...

I forgot my promise... I forgot myself...

I drowned in her eyes at once, like in a whirlpool — not bemoaning it one bit.

"Listen," her voice reached me from afar. "What's the matter with you? How are you feeling?"

"*Like I'm in heaven*," I whispered.

"Well, then, we need to go. The time has come," she pronounced the mystifying phrase. "Let's go to the park. At this moment Autumn is there holding sway. And the air is redolent with the sweet scent of dying."

The park paths were bestrewn with yellow leaves. We strolled, unhurriedly. Where to? Nowhere. Just strolled.

The trees parted into a clearing, and we emerged in front of a pond. Yellow leaves also covered the surface of the water, which rocked them gently.

We found several attractions around the pond: a house of mirrors, a shooting gallery, all sorts of carousels, a Ferris or "devil's wheel". Summer here was probably quite a cheery place. Music in the air...

But now it was late fall.

All the same, a little girl was standing on the semi-circular wooden platform, a stage. She wore a light blue dress, with a ribbon of identical blue fastened to her curls. On catching sight of us, the child curtsied and proposed:

"Would you like me to put on a concert for you?"

Without waiting for our consent, the youngster drew an imaginary curtain and started dancing to imaginary music, singing:

"La-la-la... La-la-la... La-la-la..."

When she finished, we started clapping. The child gave bows all around and, springing off the stage, ran over to us. She looked my companion over intently, all eyes.

"How are you, then, my sweet?" my new friend asked her. "Are you getting accustomed?"

"Yes, madam," the little girl replied, shyly.

"You're not missing home?"

"No, madam."

"And you're not afraid of death anymore?"

"Oh, madam!" the child cried out, and her face shone with joy. "Death is the most wonderful thing in the world."

A cold shiver ran up my back. All of sudden I didn't feel quite so snug in this autumnal park.

"Oh, Uncle Valery!" the little girl exclaimed, having noticed me. "Hi."

In that moment I recognized her, too. This was the daughter of a cousin of mine. Olga.

She'd died two years before, of a blood infection.

"Hello, Olga," I muttered.

"How's my Mommy? Do you ever visit?"

I took my companion by the elbow.

"For God's sake, let's go."

I led her away in the direction of the "devil's wheel."

"See you, Uncle Valery!" Olga called after us.

This "See you" sent another shiver down my spine.

Next to the "devil's wheel" sat a decrepit old man. As we approached he got up with difficulty and, seeing the girl, mumbled through a toothless maw:

"Hello, madam."

"Hello, my sweet," the girl replied. "So how's everything here? You're not missing home?"

"No, mistress, I don't miss it. It's so nice to die."

The girl indicated one of the wheel's little cabins nearby.

"Would you give us a ride?"

"For many, many years now nobody's ridden on the wheel," said the old man.

"We will," the girl shook her head insistently.

The old man crept into a ramshackle booth. Something inside there began loudly droning, and the "devil's wheel" slowly started to move.

I seated the girl in the cabin, climbed in myself, and we set off on our journey upwards, above the autumnal park.

"You're not afraid of heights?" she asked.

"Terribly afraid," I answered frankly. "And you?"

"Me too."

"Then let's hold hands and close our eyes," I suggested. "That way it won't be so scary."

"Let's!"

We held hands and closed our eyes. Pretending I didn't really mean to, I put my arms around her shoulders. She, also pretending she didn't mean to, pressed herself to me, eyes shut. And smiled. I looked down, expecting to see the park, the pond, the house with the columns.

THEY WERE ALL GONE WITHOUT A TRACE!

Stretching out to the very horizon was a smooth, watery surface. The "devil's wheel," slowly spinning, had its bottom half underwater. Our cabin, having already crossed the highest point, was now descending. The empty cabins below us were vanishing into the murky depths, one after another. A few more and we'd be swallowed up too. And then, a little later — after all, the wheel wasn't stopping, it kept on spinning — our drowned corpses, having made the fatal half-circle, would surface on the other side, and everything would repeat itself again and again and again...

Thus, day after day, the "devil's wheel" would spin; a school of voracious fish would anxiously look forward to its regular banquet. And very soon only a couple of skeletons, picked clean, would ride apathetically on this wheel of death that protruded desolately out of a boundless ocean.

I could see this all so clearly that trembling uncontrollably I shut my eyes again.

"That's it," echoed a resounding voice. "Hey, what're you, sleeping?"

I opened my eyes.

What the hell? The autumnal park was back. The old man sat

by the booth. And the girl was already standing in the path, her hands stretched up to the sky.

Snowflakes twirled through the air.

"Look! Look!" the girl cried. "It's the first snow! It's falling on the yellow leaves. How beautiful!" And she started making circles along with the snowflakes, as if she were one of them.

Running over to me, the girl playfully pinched my nose.

"What's the matter, you mean you really fell asleep?"

Instead of an answer, I gave her a kiss. I'm not sure myself how it happened. I just kissed her.

She didn't return my kiss. But she smiled. Sadly.

"Why's your smile so sad?" I asked.

"Guess."

I retreated half a step.

"You mean you're... You're name is..."

"Diana," she covered my mouth with her little palm. "Call me Diana. Or Denise. Whichever you prefer."

Recalling Mr. Schulz's advice, I laughed bitterly.

"Diana," I said, "or Denise, would you like me to take your picture?"

"Oh, no, don't," she wrinkled up her nose adorably. "I look terrible."

"You look beautiful." I got my camera. "Smile. Here comes the little birdie."

She smiled. But the little birdie didn't come.

We strolled along the park paths, first one, then another... The fallen leaves rustled beneath our feet. Snowflakes fell on our heads and shoulders.

Before long we walked over to the park exit — a small iron gate in a fence. On the other side of the fence stood the black car.

"Time for you to go," Denise (or Diana) said, simply.

"You're... letting me go?"

I just couldn't believe it! I couldn't!

She tousled my hair.

"You know, there's a story by Bunin, 'Cold Autumn.' In it the hero tells his beloved, just before his death: 'You live on a while, enjoy your time on earth, then come to me.' That's what I'm telling you: 'Live on a bit longer, enjoy yourself; you don't need to come to me, I myself will come to you.'"

We were silent a while. The snow fell, soundlessly.

"Can I kiss you again, one more time?" I asked. "A goodbye kiss."

She nodded.

Afterwards I got in the car. It drove off. This time in a hurry. But all the same I managed a long look at the delicate, small figure in white, slowly receding into the depths of the park.

The next day I stopped by Mr. Schulz's. He was still drinking his tea.

"So, Valery, did you end up going to that carnival at Death's place?"

"Yes, Mr. Schulz, I did."

"And made it back?"

"As you can see."

"Ma-a-arvelous... But how'd she see fit to let you leave?"

"Very simple. We got to liking each other."

"All the more reason for her not to let you go." He gulped some tea. "So, what did she... you know, look like?"

I showed him the photo.

"That's her."

"Not a bad-looking girl," said Mr. Schulz.

Back home I stuck the picture in a frame and hung it over my desk. And now, whenever I'm writing my stories out long-hand,

and then typing them up on my computer, I glance up from time to time at that cherished snapshot — from which, smiling wanly, SHE looks back at me.

BELOVED, WHEN YOU COME FOR ME I WILL MEET YOU WITH OPEN ARMS.

This is a Recorded Message

Translated by Kathleen Cook

Zaborov's wife, Katya, worked as an answering machine. She lay on the divan all day, smoking cigarettes, reading thrillers and answering the phone, whenever it rang, in a metallic voice:

"This is a recorded message. Today in such-and-such a cinema such-and-such a film is showing at such-and-such a time."

Zaborov lay on the divan next to Katya, not smoking, not reading thrillers and not answering the phone. He just lay there staring at the ceiling.

And thinking to himself all the time: "I'm staring at the ceiling."

Sometimes he went to his favourite cafe Surprise.

Last time the surprise was a dead cockroach in the salad.

This time it was a live fly in a cup of coffee.

"That's a fly," Zaborov thought.

"How ridiculous," thought the fly, floundering, "to drown in a cup of unsweetened coffee."

Zaborov fished the fly out with his finger and flicked it aside. The fly banged its head painfully on the wall and nearly fainted.

Zaborov drank the coffee and set off for the station. He had decided to go back to the town of his childhood.

The woman in the ticket office had fallen asleep with her head cupped in her hands. She dreamt that she was Cleopatra.

Zaborov woke the woman up, bought a ticket and got on the train.

The train set off. Through the window was Russia.

"That's Russia," Zaborov thought.

When night came, Zaborov was still looking at Russia, but all he could see was his faint reflection in the glass.

"That's me," he thought. "Zaborov."

Next morning Zaborov arrived at the town of his childhood. Here he had been born and here he had died.

Zaborov was not aware that he was already dead.

But this is how he was born. The chemist shop had run out of condoms, so Zaborov's father tried using a child's balloon instead. The balloon had burst at the critical moment.

But that was not all.

In those days the bookshop sold nothing but communist party brochures and manuals on pig-breeding and steel production. As she vomited over the washbasin every morning Zaborov's mother tried to figure out the cause. "It might have been the mushrooms yesterday or the tinned food the day before, but what could have caused it today, it can't be the stewed fruit, can it?"

After that Zaborov appeared and was soon sent to a nursery school.

Now time had come full circle, and Zaborov was going back to the nursery school again.

But the nursery school was not there.

On the first floor, where the playroom had been, there was now the municipal courtroom. And on the ground floor, where the bedroom had been, there was a flourishing private meat shop.

Someone was being tried in the courtroom.

In the meat shop the butcher was cutting up meat, blood spattering in all directions.

"Careful," Zaborov exclaimed. "You're splashing blood all over me!"

"You're pretty bloody already," the butcher smirked.

"He's joking," Zaborov thought.

"I'm joking," said the butcher. "But actually I have the fine, sensitive soul of a dreamer. Do you know what I would like most of all in the world?"

Zaborov didn't know.

"To be a butterfly and spend my time fluttering from flower to flower," the butcher confided. "With the forest in the distance and a little stream shining in the sunlight..."

He went silent. Zaborov was silent too. While they were silent you could hear the judge upstairs passing the death sentence.

"But instead of fluttering about, here I am hacking meat," the butcher sighed.

"There used to be a nursery school here..." Zaborov began.

"So there was," the butcher nodded. "I've got a list of all the children who went there."

He pulled out a notebook well thumbed by bloody fingers.

"There you are," he said proudly. "I kept a record of everyone. Who was who and what happened to them. It's a sort of hobby."

Zaborov's heart beat faster.

"What about... Lara Popova? Is she on your list?"

"We'll soon find out." The butcher licked a finger and flicked through the pages.

"Lara." Zaborov closed his eyes and sighed dreamily.

"... a slip of a girl in a white dress... with a big pink ribbon in her hair... and round brown eyes... the taste of the first kiss... Lara..."

"Popova," the butcher had found her. "Three divorces, four lovers, five abortions."

"Oh, no!" Zaborov groaned.

"Here's the address," the butcher smirked.

Lara was doing the washing in a tub.

"Zaborov?" she hooted, wiping her wet hands on her apron. "Well, I'll be blowed!"

"That can't be Lara. Not my Lara," Zaborov thought, looking at the shapeless middle-aged woman with a double chin.

Then they went to the cinema to see an American comedy. Everyone in the audience laughed, except Zaborov.

"How much is your income, honey?" Lara whispered in his ear.

It was snowing outside. "It's snowing," thought Zaborov.

They walked home after the cinema. Lara talked about her stomach problems. They walked along one street and then another and Lara still went on talking about her stomach problems.

"Lara," Zaborov couldn't stand it any longer. "Why do you keep talking about your stomach problems?"

Lara snorted scornfully.

"You're such a goody-goody, Zaborov."

Then they lay in bed.

Lara began to flirt.

"I gave you quite a present today," she tickled Zaborov. "Naughty boy."

"I'm the one who gave you a present," Zaborov replied limply.

"You're a pain, Zaborov!" Lara howled. "No wonder you'd been shot."

"How d'you mean?" Zaborov did not understand.

"Destroyed with an air-to-air missile during military exercise."

Zaborov didn't believe her. He went to the cemetery.

It turned out to be true. There engraved on a plain tombstone were the words:

"To our dearly beloved Vadik from Mummy and Daddy."

Zaborov's first name was, indeed, Vadik.

A young man stared out fearfully from the enamelled portrait. There was grass growing on the grave.

"So I'm dead," Zaborov thought sadly. His thoughts took on a melancholic tinge. "I'm gone, but the grass is growing..."

There was an intercity phone booth by the entrance to the cemetery.

Zaborov found a coin and dialled his home number.

"This is a recorded message..." came his wife's metallic voice.

"Katya!" Zaborov shouted down the receiver. "I'm dead! Katya!"

"Today our cinema is showing an hilarious American comedy..."

"Katya!" Zaborov sobbed down the receiver. "Katya... Katya..."

The line went dead.

Zaborov wanted to press his burning face against the cool glass. And stand like that... for a minute... and another... forever.

But all the panes of glass in the telephone booth were broken.

Beyond the cemetery he could see the forest and a stream sparkling in the sunlight. A butterfly was fluttering from flower to flower...

"The butcher," Zaborov thought.

Last Train From the Metro Station "Despair" Or A Writer of Epitaphs

Translated by José Alaniz

I live alone, and I have a cat named Yorick. Or, rather, I did until recently. He was run over by a car last fall, when Nelly the acrobat and her husband — a tiger tamer — were moving into our building.

Now it's winter.

I'm freezing. I'm always freezing, even if I put three sweaters on. I write epitaphs for a living. I get paid for it. I won't starve anytime soon since someone or other dies every day.

Some time passes, and before long spring arrives.

The snow melted fast. In the courtyard, underneath some sickly little bushes, lay the half-rotted carcass of my Yorick.

And all thanks to Nelly the acrobat moving in here.

At first she made a tremendous impression on me. In the brilliance of the floodlights, I saw a tiny girl in pink tights. She flitted gracefully about under the dome of the circus. I wanted to invite her out to a cafe, buy her ice cream... Later I learned that, by then, Nelly the acrobat was already thirty-two.

"Hello," sounded a woman's voice. "Is this your cat?"

I turned. Behind me stood Nelly the acrobat.

"Yes, it is."

"What's his name?"

"Yorick. Your husband ran him over last year."

"Poor Yorick," sighed the acrobat. "My poor husband."

"Why 'poor husband'? Did he get run over, too?"

"Worse. He got gobbled up by a tiger. Right in the middle of a show."

Nelly went on to tell me how her husband the animal tamer would, as the crowning feat of his show, stick his head in a tiger's maw. And one fine day the tiger grabbed on to his head, and snapped its jaws shut.

"A pity," I said, recalling my old wish to invite the acrobat out to a cafe.

"Do you like ice cream?" I asked.

"I like beer," answered Nelly.

So I asked her out to a beer hall.

We boarded tram No. 42. Inside, besides us, sat another couple: a little blonde of about thirty and a blond man of about fifty. Both drunk. Every time the tram made a turn, the little blonde would slouch all over her companion.

"Get wasted on your own time," she muttered.

It started raining. Drops of rain raced across the window glass.

"Tell me about yourself," Nelly asked.

I told her:

"There were two of us. Sasha and me. We went to day care together, to kindergarten together, to school together, and to air force pilot school together. We even fell in love with the same girl, Sveta, together..."

"And you married her together," Nelly added.

"No. This is when we started parting ways. Svetlana picked Sasha. They got married. Sasha and I were stationed in the same unit. One day we decided to go hunting. Sveta came with us. I lagged behind a bit. Suddenly there was a rustling in the bushes. I fired, thinking it was a hazel-grouse. But it was Sveta. I was discharged. Sasha was transferred to another unit. Sveta was buried..."

At the next turn, the blonde fell all over the blond.

"Get wasted on your own time," she complained again.

"You think I like driving you around?" the tram driver started yelling into the microphone. "Morning to night I have to take your filthy abuse! Answer your stupid questions! I'm driving around in a circle, like an ass! And I get peanuts for it!"

"Take it easy," the blond advised the driver peaceably. "Other people don't have it any better."

"I don't give a damn about other people!" the driver yelled. "I'm an artist! Can you chicken brains understand that? Ar-tist! After work I paint pictures. Sunsets and sunrises! Old men and children!"

"Well, go on and paint to your heart's content," I said, sticking my nose in. "Maybe you're the next Van Gogh."

"The next who?"

"Van Gogh. The artist, from Holland."

"No, I'm not Van Gogh. I'm the driver of tram No. 42!" he yelled hysterically. "And that's all! That's all!"

"Well, here it comes now," I thought.

But nothing came.

Because Nelly the acrobat walked up to the driver and stroked his cheek.

"Calm down, sweetheart," she said.

And the driver calmed down at once.

"Next stop: the cemetery," he announced.

Next to the cemetery was a beer hall called "The White Horse." Nelly pushed the door open, the hall was deserted. Out of the hall's murky depths emerged a robust old man with a disheveled beard. Completely drunk.

"How's business, Uncle Pasha?" Nelly the acrobat asked him.

"Business?" the old man frowned. "Ain't none. But lotsa broads still want me anyway. I only give it to some of 'em. Ha-ha-ha!" He had a powerful, booming laugh that suited his powerful figure.

"So, you came to suck on a nice foamy one?" asked Uncle Pasha.

"I did," nodded Nelly, "but he prefers ice cream." She pointed to me.

"What planet're you from, schoolboy?" he asked, menacingly. "I don't like you high-and-mighty types."

"Don't pay any attention to him," the acrobat whispered in my ear. "He's really touchy. Any little thing'll set him off, make him insult you, or beat you..."

Uncle Pasha brought over some snacks and drinks on a tray.

"Let's down a few, schoolboy," he muttered, pouring vodka into three glasses. "I like you, son."

Like all drunks, his mood turned on a dime.

"Drink up," advised Nelly.

I drank.

Uncle Pasha, slumping all over me, breathing in my face:

"You gotta treat women like they was your sister, schoolboy."

"Get away from me," I pushed him aside.

Uncle Pasha scrunched up my shirt collar.

"Gimme a hunnert!" he demanded, in a tone which boded ill. "C'mon!"

I gave him a hundred rubles.

"I'll pay ya back," he promised.

"No doubt."

Uncle Pasha again poured us all some vodka. We drank up.

"We're gonna get nice and hammered," he said contentedly.

Very soon I was drunk. My cheeks burned.

"Nelly," I looked at her ruefully. "I have this feeling that my life ended a long, long time ago. But I just keep on living... I walk along the streets. I see people. They're all saying something, talking, talking... Sometimes I just want to stamp my feet and start yelling: 'Shut up! Shut up!' And other times I want to drown myself in some forest lake. Just let myself sink down to the sandy bottom, and lie there, and watch the seaweed swaying, the fish frolicking... And you, Nelly, have you ever wanted to just drown yourself?"

"And how, schoolboy," butted in Uncle Pasha.

"I spend a lot of time at home," I went on, ignoring him. "I sit and draw little black and white squares. And little human half-faces. For some reason it's always just half-faces."

"You avant-garde, you," grunted Uncle Pasha, knocking back another shot.

But I was carried away:

"Very often, Nelly, I simply shut myself off from the world. I don't read the papers, I don't watch T.V. I sleep or just lie in bed. And later, when I come back to this stupid world, I see that nothing has changed. No-thing. Well, of course, some things do change," I corrected myself. "But essentially... essentially..."

"Essench'ly," Uncle Pasha chimed in, "we's like roaches in a can: we gobble each other up, an' don't take down no names, neither."

"Will you shut up!" I couldn't contain myself.

"Wha-whassat?" Uncle Pasha rose in threat.

"Sit down," ordered Nelly the acrobat.

Uncle Pasha sat down.

"Okay, schoolboy," he grumbled. "We'll let this one pass fer now, but later on..." He wanted to add something, but right then his jaw dropped and his eyebrows shot up. "Nelly," he mumbled, goggling at the acrobat, "they said you'd died..."

"I died, I died," Nelly the acrobat started laughing. "Who doesn't?"

Uncle Pasha feverishly poured himself more vodka, drank it, poured some more, drank that too... Then his head sank down onto the table.

As for me, it was like someone had unfolded a newspaper before my eyes. I saw the headline:

"DEATH OF A TALENTED CIRCUS ACROBAT!"

"You're dead?" I whispered in shock.

"Do you have a cigarette?" said Nelly in response.

I handed her one. Nelly stuck it into a white cigarette holder, and started smoking. And the strangest thing: this ordinary gesture had the most disconcerting effect on me.

"How did it happen?" I asked.

Nelly blew a tiny smoke ring.

"Very simple. While we were on tour in Sochi, I fell off the trapeze. It was a good five stories down. I can imagine how I looked in the coffin."

"But..." I stammered.

"What?"

"But how can you be here?" I gasped.

Nelly blew another little ring. She laughed.

"It only looks like I'm here. But I'm really not."

"Well, where are you? In the afterlife?"

"Naturally," she confirmed. "After all, I'm dead."

Words were spoken. And... and nothing. The drunk Uncle Pasha snored. Beneath the ceiling a fly buzzed. We went on talking quietly.

"You know what I like best of all about the theater?" I asked. "When all the actors come out for their bows. Those who were killed during the play, along with those who weren't. They take each other by the hand, step up to the edge of the stage, and bow. And the audience claps and gives them flowers. They're all alive and healthy, and now they'll go home, for dinner..."

"A-ah, so," said the acrobat, with a knowing laugh, "you're afraid that maybe you'll want to come back?"

"What do you m..." I began, and immediately realized just *what* the what was, and added, "Yes. I am afraid."

"But you have decided, for good?" she looked me in the eyes, inquisitively.

I wasn't sure *how* I'd decided.

"Ha-ha-ha!" Uncle Pasha raised his head up off the table. "I went to the theater once. 'Bout twenty years ago. The play was called, 'It's Good to be the Under-Secretary.' Get it? Under the secretary."

"We get it," I said.

Uncle Pasha returned his head to the table.

"Have you ever heard of the station 'Despair'?" asked Nelly, after a pause.

"'Despair'?" I repeated. "No, I haven't. Where is it?"

"In 'Moskovskaya.'"

"In what 'Moskovskaya'?"

"In the metro station 'Moskovskaya,'" she explained. "It's odd you don't know it. Everybody who's gotten tired of life knows about this place. 'Moskovskaya' is the station 'Despair.' You just have to board the last carriage of the last train..."

"And then what?"

"And nothing. You wind up *there.*"

I laughed.

"The metro construction workers dug a tunnel all the way to the next world?"

"No, they didn't. Someone on his way to another destination arrives at that other destination. But people who fully intend to commit suicide create a particular aura around themselves... a certain field... I can't explain it in words. Or rather, I could, of course, but it wouldn't come out right. In short, whoever wants to ride away to death — rides away."

Cheeks in palms, I struggled to comprehend the situation. At times it felt like I had fallen into some kind of impenetrable darkness, where only voices were heard.

"Have you read Nabokov, Uncle Pasha?" asked Nelly in a playful voice.

"No, I have not," answered the voice of Uncle Pasha, gallantly. "Reading Nabokov's the same as sleepin' with a dead woman."

"I read books too!" I screamed.

And at my scream the damned murk fell away, slowly spilling out onto the floor, like black fog. The bar re-emerged. And Nelly the acrobat was looking at me with eyes full of pity.

I rushed — rushed! — to tell her:

"You know, Nelly, a while ago I read a biography of Isadora Duncan. One time she was riding in an open car. Her long scarf got caught up in the wheel and strangled the brilliant dancer. And now there's no more Isadora Duncan! And no Dostoyevsky! And no Leo Tolstoy! And no Napoleon! God, how many have there been who've ceased to exist! But me, I do exist!"

"And me too, I exist!" wailed Uncle Pasha.

"You existing doesn't mean a thing," coldly noted the acrobat, and fell silent. But her words kept hovering over our heads, like cigarette smoke.

"Nelly," I mumbled pitiably, laying my flushed cheek on the cold marble table, "life is killing me with its monotony. These endless repetitions would drive anyone insane. Nelly, life is a chain of repetitions..."

"Right you are, schoolboy!" thundered Uncle Pasha, slapping me on the back. "It's a hard thing, life!"

And this time his lack of ceremony didn't annoy me.

"Yes, yes," I found myself agreeing with him, "Life's a hard thing. Especially when you're past forty and you've started off on the second round."

God, what was all this? The damned beer hall hung over me and was pressing, pressing down, like a tombstone... I was suffocating... And in disarray, I got up from the table, and ran, ran...

"How about a smoke?" Uncle Pasha took me by the arm. "We can do that with gr-rreat pleasure."

And here we were already, out on the street, having a smoke. A cold wind cooled my burning face. But my head was no clearer.

Things weren't any clearer.

Nelly the acrobat kindheartedly suggested:

"You need to apologize to this beloved girl of yours. Things didn't turn out too well, you can't deny that..."

I didn't deny it.

A black sky hung over us. It hung sort of sideways, irritatingly. And the bright stars dazzled my eyes with their dead light.

Two military jets roared by.

"Air raid!" Uncle Pasha let out with a heart-rending cry, and threw himself to the ground.

"Stop clowning," frowned Nelly.

"You can't even make a joke anymore," grumbled Uncle Pasha, getting up and dusting himself off.

I began weeping and sobbing, in shudders.

"Nelly... I'm so alone... So sad... Nelly... I murdered my love..."

"It's alright, sweetheart, it's alright," she stroked my cheek. "It's nothing that can't be fixed." And, turning to Uncle Pasha, she said: "Time for us to go."

"Don't let me keep you," he started bustling about. "Thank you for coming by. It was nice to meet you." He came up to me for a goodbye kiss. "Well, take it easy, schoolboy. Remember what

Chekhov wrote about Pushkin: 'On the stage, the three sisters and Uncle Vanya.' In other words: *femine more anime*. Don't let broads get the best of you, schoolboy! Got it?"

We set off for the metro station "Moskovskaya." It was a ten-minute walk. It was still possible to change things. But suddenly I was seized by a feeling of absolute indifference. "A-ah..." I thought. And that's all.

We took the escalator down to the station "Despair." At first sight it was clear what sort of people gathered there. By the wall stood a little girl in tears. A pallid old man sat on a bench. A young girl, biting her lips, paced the platform desolately.

At the platform's edge I saw the driver of tram No. 42.

"You decided to... leave, too?" I asked him.

He didn't answer, but kept on peering nervously at the black opening of the tunnel.

A train pulled in. We went into the last carriage.

"Attention, the doors are closing," droned the loudspeaker. *And the doors closed.*

In about two minutes we arrived.

It was already fall there. It was raining.

"Stop crossing!" yelled a policeman into a megaphone, standing at a crossroads. "Can't you see the light's red!"

"Wow," I said in amazement. "Everything's like in that other world."

"This *is* the other world," Nelly shrugged.

We went to a train station. I bought a ticket. The train was leaving in one minute. We crossed over to the platform.

The rain stopped. It started snowing.

"Alright, then," said Nelly. "In case anything happens, you know who to turn to."

"Who?" I asked, not understanding.

"God. Who else?"

"I'll be back soon," I promised.

She shook her head.

"You're never going back. Here you can't ever go back."

"Okay, okay, see ya," I said, as casually as possible. "I'm going on a long trip, but my heart's staying right here with you."

Nelly said nothing.

I got in the carriage and took my seat. Nelly had already left the platform. Leaning back, I closed my eyes.

The train set off.

"How ya doing, asshole?" echoed a familiar-sounding bass, right in my ear.

Next to me sat... Uncle Pasha.

"How did you get here?" I goggled at him in disbelief.

"Easy as can be, schoolboy," he grinned. "I up and croaked! But what're *you* doing here, a young man, full'a interesting things to look forward to? I told ya: don't give in to broads!"

"I don't give a damn!" I declared, defiantly.

"Don't give a damn about what?"

"About anything!"

"There's a bum for ya!" barked Uncle Pasha in delight. "Where ya off to?"

"Nowhere. Just taking a ride."

"Well, then, I'll tag along. Pay my respects."

"First pay me those hundred rubles."

All of sudden Uncle Pasha's face went bluish-white, like the color of tin.

"You scumbag, don't you trust Uncle Pasha?"

"I trust you," I said, and quickly moved to the next carriage.

"Ladies and gentlemen!" Uncle Pasha started bawling out after me. "Preserve the Russian classics! Don't lose sight of God!"

The little town didn't look like anything special. Smoke puffed out of some factory smokestacks. A little church clung to a hill. Oddly, there was even a cemetery.

Crows cawed.

An old bus rumbled up to the stop. Behind the wheel sat the former driver of tram No. 42.

"I went to see Van Gogh," he happily reported. "He advised me to keep on with my painting."

"Congratulations," I said.

We set off.

On either side of the road stood a dense forest. The bus was barely moving. "God, why are we just dragging along like this?" I asked myself in irritation.

"And where do we need to hurry to anymore?" answered the former driver of tram No. 42, as if he'd read my mind. "Up ahead is Eternity."

We passed one small village, a second, a third; dogs barked, children ran about, old men sat on porches. And again forest... forest... forest...

At last, after crossing a checkpoint, the bus entered an air base. My best friend Sasha had lived here once, and my beloved Sveta. I had lived here, too.

Sveta wasn't surprised to see me.

"Sasha's here, too," she reported. "He died in a crash a year after you shot me."

"You live together?"

"We did, for two years. Then we got divorced. And how'd your life go?"

"Oh, nothing special. They discharged me from the army. I worked in a factory. Then I sold newspapers. Then I wrote epitaphs."

"And your poetry? Did you publish anything?"

"Yeah. A quatrain in a journal:

> *Though Lisa's gone*
> *No one's sadder in the face*
> *But Lisa's gone*
> *So the world's another place.*"

"Nice," she said.

"I stole it from some English poet," I confessed. "My own poetry never made it into print."

"And did you have a wife, kids?" asked Sveta.

"No, I didn't."

A clock was ticking on the sideboard. Rain pounded on the window.

"Poor, poor epitaph-writer," she said tenderly. "Did you do yourself in?"

"Well... Sort of, yeah."

Later we sat in her kitchen. Had tea. I looked at this girl, whom I had loved unrequited twenty years before. She hadn't changed a bit. She was still the same eighteen-year-old.

"I'm sorry that back then I... killed you," I said. "I don't understand myself how it happened. 'Til then I'd never fired blind, at a rustling sound. And then this..."

"It's alright," Sveta waved the remark away. "What's the point of bringing it up now?"

It started to get dark. I stood up.

"Guess I'll be on my way."

Svetlana walked me to the bus stop. The same old bus rolled up. The former driver of tram No. 42 opened the door.

"All aboard," he announced.

"See you," I told Sveta.

"We don't say 'see you' here," she replied, with a sad smile. "Here we say, 'Farewell.' "

"Farewell," I said.

Taman

Translated by José Alaniz

Taman is the nastiest little town of all the coastal towns in Russia. I went there in early spring of 1953. It was a slow train, it stopped a lot, bestowing on me the dubious privilege of admiring at leisure the small, crisscrossing wooden houses, old women in shapeless jersies and army boots, and emaciated cows grazing the tired grass on the railway embankment.

Then the train would slowly start moving. The old cars would begin rumbling down the wobbly rails.

I lay on the lower bunk, looking through the compartment's open door and out the corridor window. What else was there to do? From my prone position I caught sight of treetops flowing by, a wire with crows perched on it, and a fragment of gray sky. Occasionally the train conductor — a fat, vulgar mamma would stop up the entrance to the compartment with her copious behind, asking playfully, "Wouldn't you like some tea-by weeby?" and slo-o-owly run the tip of her tongue along lips thickly smeared with lipstick. "No, thank you," I'd answer, adding to myself, "Old bitch!"

The train dragged itself into Taman only by evening. An hour late, no less. Passing a monument to Stalin all done up in gilt, I walked into the waiting area. In there hung two more enormous portraits of him and still another monument. Also in there a pretty girl dressed in the latest fashion sat on a bench smoking. Not far from her, sitting right on the floor, was a blind boy of about fourteen, in a filthy white shirt. When I passed by, he pathetically drawled:

"Uncle, give us some change."

"Beat it," I said.

The pretty girl, without even smoking her cigarette halfway, spat it out onto the floor. The blind boy grabbed it up and puffed greedily.

"Fuck a duck!" said the pretty girl. "One fine day I decide not to take a taxi and go on the metro. And what do you know... I get off at the Lermontov station like a good girl and wind up in the men's bathroom of this damn train station. Can you tell me where I am, exactly?"

"This is Taman," I said, "the nastiest little town of all the coastal towns in Russia."

"Taman?" the girl got another cigarette out of the pack.

"Yes," I nodded. "Taman."

"Cool," she lighted another cigarette. "And is there a bar here?"

I shrugged.

"Hey, paisano!" the girl called out to the blind boy. "Is there a bar around here?"

"Ha, ha, ha," the blind boy cackled senselessly.

"Right," said the girl. "Idiot!"

Her name was Mary. We went in search of a restaurant. The blind boy shuffled after us.

The moon sailed through the sky.

Soon we saw a neon sign: it was the restaurant "The White Hole." I knocked on the door. A huge bouncer bald as a billiard ball looked out. I christened him Shaggy — to myself.

"We're closed!" he snapped rudely.

Mary pulled a couple of dollar bills out of her little purse and waved them under his nose.

Shaggy thoughtfully scratched his bald head and let us in.

In the checkroom sat a gloomy old man with the face of a bulldog. He wore a black jacket, black tie and black shirt. You could've just dragged him as is straight to the graveyard. Next to him sat a well-fed black cat.

"Ooh, kitty!" Mary erupted in that moronic tone that all women use to talk to pets and children. "What a furry one! And what's your name?"

"Don't bother the cat," said the old man sullenly. "She doesn't like it."

As if to underscore this statement, the black cat languidly got up, stretched and sidled off.

"That's Maxim Maximich," cheerfully explained Shaggy. "Our in-house necrorealist artist. He draws only dead bodies. So, whenever you kick the bucket, you can order your own portrait from him."

We passed into a small round hall. At one of the tables sat a neatly dressed young man. He half rose, bowed in our direction and introduced himself:

"Nemukhin. Nice to meet you." And sat back down.

We sat down too. On our little table stood a tiny nightlight with a red shade. Mary pressed the button. The light came on. It got cozy.

The atmosphere lent itself to intimacy.

"Mary," I said, "what's your real name, honestly?"

"Honestly," said Mary, "it's Sonya."

"Marmeladova?"

"Tomatova!"

I tickled her behind the right ear.

"Meow," said Sonya and closed her eyes.

"Don't bother the cat!" Maxim Maximich angrily yelled out from behind the door. "She doesn't like it!"

"Sonya," I said with a heavy sigh. "I love you. How much do you cost?"

"I love you too," answered Sonya. "But I'm a good girl, that's why I cost so much."

A waiter came up to us.

"And what'll we be having?" he blithely asked.

"What've you got?" I asked in his same tone.

"There's a Chinese dish made of three fragrances. We hired a Chinaman from Beijing. Mr. Yu. He'll make it for you. But I gotta warn you, it ain't cheap."

"And what else is there?"

"Well, there's noodles, too," he said dully. "Yesterday's noodles."

"We'll have the noodles."

"No, what for?" Sonya thrust herself into our conversation. "Let's have your house dish."

The waiter, satisfied, ran off.

"By the way, Sonya," I asked, "why do you wear watches on both wrists?"

"I've got 'em on my ankles, too," she coquettishly bent her little head to the side.

I crawled under the table to personally verify.

And indeed, a Zarya watch was ticking away over the black licra hose on her right ankle, while on her left I saw some foreign make. With a glowing dial.

The blind boy sat under the next table, stroking the black cat.

I myself stroked Sonya's legs, just above the knee.

"Uh, u-u-uh," said Sonya.

Shaggy's worried face peeped under the table.

"Excuse me," said his face, "but Mr. Yu wants you to come to the kitchen right away."

I reluctantly got up, dusting off my pants.

In the kitchen, by the stove, stood someone who was either Japanese or Chinese. Short. Old. In a dirty apron.

"Here, I brought 'im," Shaggy reported gloomily, pointing me out.

Mr. Yu introduced himself and launched into a long monologue: "One day I was riding metro in Beijing. As always, it was packed. Suddenly, I saw beautiful woman. And she saw me. We stared into each other's eyes long time. Then some force expelled me from the carriage. The train went on. I realized that that woman had been my wife in previous life. At that time we had made each other unhappy. I was seized by feeling of complete irreparableness. I abandoned my restaurant, my wife and children, and came to your country. But here too I cannot find peace of mind."

"And what do you want from me?" I asked.

"I want you to help me. I want to perform hara-kiri now..."

It just what I need, I thought in a funk.

"... according to ancient Japanese custom, servant is present during hara-kiri. And when master disembowels himself, servant asks him, 'Do you need assistance, sir?' Because no death is more excruciating than hara-kiri. Not everyone can withstand such horrendous pain. And if master says, 'Help me,' then servant lops off his head with long samurai sword."

Mr. Yu retrieved a long samurai sword, with a hilt fit for two hands, from under the stove.

I must have grown pale visibly.

"But you're, if you'll excuse me, a Chinaman," I pathetically started to babble. "And hara-kiri, if memory serves, is a custom of the Japanese."

"Mr. Yu is a Chinaman of Japanese ancestry," explained Shaggy, who up 'til then had maintained a tomblike silence. "He's the descendant of an ancient samurai clan and..."

"Leave it," Mr. Yu said weightily. "Right now we're talking

about something else." His narrow little eyes resumed boring into my face. "Get ahold of yourself," Mr. Yu said quietly, extending me the sword.

I got ahold of myself. After all, what's it to me?

"Fine," I said. "Go ahead if you must!"

Mr. Yu pulled out of his apron pocket a small dagger with a long, straight edge. Then he stared at his stomach...

"I better spread out a rag or something," Shaggy prudently fussed. "Or else you'll stain everything with blood."

Mr. Yu said nothing, his eyes still fixed on his stomach...

We waited.

I squeezed hard on the sword hilt.

But then the door burst open, and Sonya walked in.

"What's going on here?" she said with irritation, "d'you want to leave me there to starve?" She froze, cutting herself off in mid-sentence. "I don't get your joke," Sonya said, catching sight of Mr. Yu with a dagger, me with a razor-sharp sword, and Shaggy with a rag in his hands.

Shaggy, in two shakes, filled her in on what we were doing.

"But what for?" she went on, still not getting it.

So Mr. Yu set about explaining it all himself.

"My soul is filled with feeling of complete irreparableness," he explained, this time succinctly. "Scientifically-speaking, this is called mental claustrophobia."

"Oh Go-od," said Sonya, making a wry face. "Every other person in Russia's got the same thing. So what? We get by. We're not slicing our guts out!"

"That's reasonable," noted Shaggy, jabbing a finger at Sonya.

Mr. Yu plunged into deep thought. And remained pensive for some ten minutes. We patiently awaited his return to reality.

Finally, he solemnly declared:

"If you're not sure about whether or not to do something, it's better not to do it," he didactically raised his index finger. "So ancient Eastern wisdom says."

Shaggy backed him up right away.

"If you're not sure whether to drink or not to drink," he said, "better not to drink!"

Sonya backed Shaggy up.

"If you're not sure whether to screw or not," she said, "better not screw!"

I backed Sonya up.

"If you're not sure whether you should write 'Taman' or not, better not write it!"

And, resolving the matter for us all, Maxim Maximich backed us all up from the checkroom.

"If you're not sure whether to be or not to be," he said philosophically, "better not to be!"

"Very well," said Mr. Yu and put the dagger away. "End of discussion. For some reason, I'm not inclined to commit hara-kiri today."

"Right! You'll do it next time," Shaggy nodded approvingly. "But right now how about making that dish with three fragrances."

"It's already done," Mr. Yu suddenly remembered, and pulled the lid off a huge cauldron on the stove.

It stank to high heaven.

I bulleted out the first door into the corridor.

The gloomy Maxim Maximich livened up a bit and offered:

"Would you like me to tell you a nice, cheerful story?"

"No!"

But he went ahead anyway: "When I was a young lad more than anything else I liked to visit cemeteries..."

I shut my eyes and was transported into a parallel world.

...I dreamt that I was drowning in a swamp: a revolting, vile-smelling slush, recalling the dish of three fragrances; squishing and squelching, it sucked me into itself. It pulled on my legs. I tasted brackish water on my lips. Meanwhile, all around, it was a nice sunny day. Not a cloud in the sky. A forest nearby was full of white birches, flower heads swaying in the wind, butterflies fluttering their wings. The sun lovingly warmed them... And me being swallowed up...

I came to just in time. Maxim Maximich was finishing his story.

"And that's that," he was saying, his aged eyes welling up with tears. "Now I'm 65, life has passed me by, and I didn't get anything worthwhile out of it. All that's left, really, in my life is two grand events: retirement and my own funeral..."

That's what his nice, cheerful stories were like.

"Yeah," I said.

"'Yeah' what?" asked Maxim Maximich.

"Never mind," I said and returned to the hall.

Sonya, Mr.Yu, Shaggy and the neatly dressed young man were finishing up the dish from three fragrances.

On the next table, rolled up in a ball, slept the black cat. Under the table, the blind boy was snoring.

When I walked up, the neatly dressed young man bowed in my direction and introduced himself:

"Nemukhin. Nice to meet you."

"So we've heard," I said.

"Anyway, he's some guy!" Shaggy thrust out his big finger.

"Are you a Japanese of Chinese ancestry too?" I asked.

"Pardon me, no," said Nemukhin humbly. "You see, I'm a family counselor. And you, do you have a wife?"

"I do," I said, "but it'd be better if I didn't."

"Well, there you are! Then I can help!" Nemukhin lit up.

He pulled out a neat little file folder and opened it.

"So, how would you like it, so that she didn't exist at all?" he beamed at me through his eyeglasses.

"No, not 'at all,'" I laughed. "But more like, she'd be sort of there" — I paused — "and sort of not there."

"Understood," said Nemukhin, as if to himself. "Instruction No. 14: Placement of wife in mental home."

"It won't work," I said confidently. "She's so smart, the pest, you start telling her something, she interrupts you and corrects you..."

"You don't understand," Nemukhin smiled sweetly. "It's precisely the smart ones that are the easiest to make into idiots..."

And he handed me a sheet of paper covered with tiny writing.

"Read it out loud," Shaggy said. "It might come in handy for me, too."

I read:

"Instruction No. 14: Placement of wife in mental home.

Buy a kilogram of nails in a hardware store and set about making repairs to your home. In the most natural, relaxed tone inform your wife that, in order to hammer the nails into the wall, they must first be tempered. For this purpose, one should place a big frying pan on an electric stove, pour some oil in it and then the nails. Tell your wife the nails must be tempered for at least an hour, stirring them constantly with a fork. As soon as your wife begins, call up the nuthouse and tell them your wife has lost her mind: she's frying up nails on the stove. Remember, you should speak in a very upset voice. From this point on your direct participation is not needed. A consultation on questions of family life guarantees the complete success of this venture, provided you follow these instructions to the letter."

"Co-o-l," Sonya drawled in delight, "Simple and smart."

"And what if they find out truth and let her out after couple of days?" Mr. Yu skeptically hemmed. "What then?"

"They won't," said Nemukhin with conviction. "As a foreigner you simply don't understand the specifics of Russian life. It's easy for anyone to land in a nuthouse. But it's not so easy to get out..." — he spread his arms.

"That's for sure," confirmed Shaggy.

"Well then, thanks," I said, with feeling. "I'll give it a try."

"If you please," Nemukhin's eye dulled over. "That'll be three rubles for the service."

"Co-o-o-l," Sonya repeated, rocking on her chair.

"Now Maxim Maximich's gonna barge in," Shaggy said all of a sudden.

And indeed Maxim Maximich barged in bearing a banged-up transistor radio.

"The latest news," he said, "Maybe somebody died."

BAM! BAM! BAM! — the Kremlin chimes sounded.

"Midnight," said the radio announcer. "The latest news..."

Maxim Maximich was right: some famous rock star settled his bill with life.

"He was driving his car, lost control of it and sud..." She unexpectedly cut off in mid-syllable.

"She's having a little drink on the job," guessed Sonya.

"... and now let's listen to his last song."

"Right!" said Maxim Maximich with satisfaction. "Driving a car ain't like strumming a guitar."

The blind boy woke up and walked over to our table.

"Gimme money!" he said, staring me in the face with hatred.

"Give him some money," advised Nemukhin. "Or else he'll throw a fit."

"Gimme money!!!" howled the blind boy, already starting to throw his fit.

I grabbed an open bottle of mineral water and thrust it into his sweaty palms. The blind boy calmed down, fastened his own drooling mouth to the bottle's and drank greedily, taking big gulps.

A phone rang in the corridor.

"Excuse me," said Shaggy and walked out.

In a minute he ran back into the room. He looked like he'd seen a ghost.

"Comrades!" he cried out, his voice breaking. "Stalin's dead!"

Sonya, losing her balance, crashed down to the floor along with her chair.

"Thank God," she responded from the floor. "He croaked, the dog! That pockmarked fucker!"

Shaggy's eyes wavered. He reeled backwards. And ran back into the corridor.

"He's going to have all of you jailed," explained Maxim Maximich.

"Jailed, shmailed," said Sonya and got up from the floor.

"You know what I'm thinking of right now?" Mr. Yu uttered pensively.

"No, we don't," I said.

"I'm thinking, that if even one person suffers, then what's use of this world?"

Shaggy returned.

"Did you snitch on us?" Sonya asked calmly.

"Yes, they're on their way," he responded. And added with pride: "Any patriot in my position would have done the same. Vigilance and more vigilance! Got it?"

"Yeah," said Sonya. "We're not stupid."

There was an uncomfortable silence.

Shaggy started nervously circling the table.

"I used to work as a lifeguard," he said, speaking quickly. "It was always stuffy around the pool... Stuffy... So I would climb up my ten-meter watch-tower, right up under the roof, where it was cooler. And I would sleep there. Then later I'd jump down into the water. This contrast — from warm sleep to cold water... It's inexpressibly good... Once I jumped down like that. I'm in the air and I see that they've drained the water out of the pool. There was maybe 50-60 centimeters left, and draining away by the second. In that instant I understood that a man only gets one life to live. And he has to live it in such a way as..."

"Skip this bit," I said. "Go on..."

"At the very last second I managed to go into swallow-dive. I slammed into what was left of that water with my chest and stomach. I wound up with a first-degree burn and worker's disability. So here I am — chucked out! And now to top it off, I'm a snitch!"

Shaggy started to cry, covering his face with his hands. Sonya hugged him. She pressed him firmly to her chest.

"It's alright, it's alright," she said tenderly, stroking his back. "You'll be fine..."

"You all hear sea waves roaring?" said Mr. Yu.

We pricked up our ears.

The sea roared...

"No!" Shaggy tore himself away from Sonya's embrace. And banged his fists on the table! "Sonya!" cried Shaggy, and in a frenzy he ripped his shirt collar. "Sonya! I'm a scoundrel! I have a motor boat! Let's start a new life together! Let's take my boat right now, and run away to Turkey! While there's still a fog! Tomorrow — we'll be there!!!"

"No!" said Sonya in her turn, quietly but firmly. "I won't leave my motherland. Especially not in a moment of bifurcation. I'm a Soviet hooker — and proud of it!"

Nemukhin exultantly rose from his seat. Tears shimmered in his eyes.

"Remember what the poet said," he cried out in rapture, "'We should make nails out of these people, then there'd be no stronger nails in the world!' He had you in mind, Sonya!"

"But what exactly is bifurcation?" I asked.

"A term in catastrophe theory," a calm voice answered for Sonya. "A precisely measured point, after which a process might proceed in several directions."

The blind boy sauntered over to our table.

"I *thought* he'd be from the Secret Service," whispered Shaggy with deadened lips.

"Move it," the blind boy ordered me.

I jumped up. He took my seat.

Taking his time, he undid the shiny clasps on a black portfolio. He took out a gray folder and a pencil. He cleared the table in front of him.

On the folder was written: "Protocol for interrogation of prisoners." On the upper left-hand corner it said: "Keep in perpetuity."

"So," he said, pointing the sharp pencil at Sonya's eye. "Profession?! Party affiliation?! Views?!"

"Hooker! Young Communist League! Liberal!" Sonya enunciated jauntily.

"Ri-i-ight," drawled the blind boy maliciously, writing it down. "Next."

I quietly slipped out into the corridor. Next to the telephone, on a little warped table, was the telephone book. A thick book with a brown cover. I feverishly began leafing through it. But instead of phone numbers the book listed the subscribers' ages and details of their deaths.

Some familiar names turned up.

The first I found was Nemukhin. He completed a correspondence course through the institute of international relations and was made ambassador to an African republic on the path to socialist transformation.

Nothing foretold his bloody end...

As it turned out the locals ate Nemukhin. This happened in 1960. During a holiday to celebrate the start of the rainy season, they cooked and devoured him. And it wasn't some reactionaries that did it, but the very ones that were progressively-minded fighters against Apartheid. Naturally, there was a note from the Soviet government, to which the president of the African republic blithely replied, "You may take two of our diplomats and eat them, too." Thus the incident was settled. But this hardly did Nemukhin any good.

Shaggy wouldn't have much luck either.

He shot clear up into the air in 1973. Together with a railroad bridge. It so happened that his favorite pastime was tossing lighted matches from the bridge onto the roofs of passing trains. There wasn't anything special about this, if you think about it. A lot of people, for example, enjoy spitting from the bridge. Well, Shaggy liked to toss burning matches. But one time a train passing under the bridge happened to be transporting some tanks of gasoline. The hatch on one of these tanks happened to be open. A flaming match happened to fall right into it.

For the other characters in this story the end wasn't quite so romantic.

Sonya, for instance, would be found dead in a filthy room in a Paris hotel in 1956. God knows how she happened to be in Paris.

Mr. Yu went off to plough up the virgin lands of Siberia and fell under a hay mower in 1958.

I found myself in the book as well. I was shot in early Spring, 2037, in one of the newly-built concentration camps in Vorkuta.

As for what ever happened to Maxim Maximich and the poor blind boy — I do not know. There wasn't a word about them in the book.

In the morning came the opportunity to move on, and so I took my leave of Taman. Never to return there.

Where Wanes the Rosy World

Translated by José Alaniz

I

Fanny Borovskaya, a thirty-four-year-old peroxide blonde, had buried her husband. The evening after the funeral she switched off the lights in her apartment, put on a disc with songs by Marilyn Monroe (Fanny liked "Hurt Me" best of all) and began swaying to the beat of the music.

Fanny was, as the saying goes, not everybody's cup of tea. Pale face, riveting eyes and bright lips that looked like they'd been smeared with blood.

Her husband, until his untimely demise, had worked as a manager of some dubious firm, which repainted cars. To tell the truth, he didn't just die, in the literal sense of the word; Fanny shot him.

He'd been getting on her nerves lately. For example, he'd come home from work and immediately go down on all fours, behaving like a Pekinese. He'd run from room to room, yelping happily, eat out of a dish (insisting it be placed right by the wash bucket), bring Fanny her house slippers in his teeth, adore it when she scratched him behind the ears... And all this, in principle, would have been entirely tolerable; after all, who doesn't have his quirks? But there's a limit to everything.

One fine day her husband flatly refused to speak, and only yapped and whimpered. And when Fanny tried to force him to say at least one word in human language, he viciously bit her on the thigh.

Without much ado Fanny got a five-shooter revolver out of the drawer, an old model (short-barreled, .38 caliber), and plugged all five bullets into her mad husband. She found it a simple matter to convince the young investigator that this had been some competitors' bloody revenge.

When the music finished, Fanny drew the curtains and flopped onto the sofa. Fanny loved the dark. In the darkness she felt safer than in artificial — to say nothing of natural — light.

Fanny took a long swig from a bottle of champagne. She went into uncontrollable fits of laughter when she remembered her late Pekinese-husband. "Sh-h-h..." she pressed a small finger to her lips. "They might hear. They're close by, already."

After luxuriating a bit more on her sofa, Fanny leapt up and rushed over to the kitchen, where she dropped onto all fours before a clean enamel dish filled with milk (she'd tossed her husband's dirty dish into the garbage chute) and, sticking out her little pink tongue, started greedily lapping up milk. The milk had already soured; the taste brought Fanny an odd mix of satisfaction and disgust.

Having drunk her fill, she lightly jumped up onto the wide window-sill, and from there, through the upper window specially opened in advance... And from there it was just one jump to the next building's roof.

Once on the roof, Fanny had herself a nice, delicious stretch. It was this moment of transformation that she loved best of all. She was seized by a sharp sensation of the fullness of life, from the ends of her ears to the fluffy tip of her tail... Yes! Fanny was a cat! That was yet another reason why she'd shot her husband (the main reason, in fact): he hadn't just been pretending to be a dog — in his essence he was a dog. While Fanny, like any normal cat, hated dogs with a passion.

Towards dawn Fanny returned home. Tired, hungry and happy. Having completely satisfied her lust. She climbed into her bathtub and lay there a long time, not moving, with her eyes closed. Basking in the clouds of steam.

When Fanny went into the bedroom, she suddenly had a sensation that it was Christmas Eve. A strange glow filled the room, like the glow from the many-colored lights on a Christmas tree (though there was in fact no tree and no lights). Fanny was seized by a wild rapture. Spreading her hands, she circled the room. Then suddenly stopped. "Sh-sh-sh..." she told herself, putting a finger to her lips. "They're here."

II

At the very moment when Fanny had fallen asleep, Makarov in the next apartment had woken up.

He was a writer, about fifty, who had rather let himself go. Curious misfortunes had haunted him. His five-year-old daughter had disappeared. (They never found her.) Another time the body of Makarov's wife was carried out of the apartment.

So, Makarov woke up.

He groped about the coffee table for a cigarette and brushed up against the alarm clock, which fell to the floor. The ticking stopped. In the courtyard a dog was howling. "Today someone's going to die for sure," thought Makarov. "Maybe even me." He got out of bed and went to the bathroom to rinse his face. "Time has stopped," he said to his reflection in the mirror. "Time has cracked."

In the city were five other mirrors in which Makarov regularly caught sight of himself. Two of them he liked, two he didn't. And the fifth one he simply detested. This mirror was in a public toilet, near the beer joint Makarov frequented. His immoderate love of beer thus made it impossible for him to avoid this unpleasant spectacle. Every time he stepped into that toilet he was forced to confront his own distorted reflection, with its gray disheveled hair.

Makarov came back to his room. The alarm clock still lay there, on the floor. From the icon of Saint Seraphim hanging in the corner, a naked girl smiled impertinently. "The day's starting off badly," thought Makarov in anguish. "Very badly." He was again seized by a presentiment of imminent death. He took up the telephone receiver and dialed the automated time service. There was a grave-like silence on the line.

Sticking a clean sheet of paper in the typewriter, Makarov started pounding on the keys in a frenzy. The broken typewriter rattled, like a machine gun. "Time has cracked," typed Makarov. "And all sorts of vermin and beasts have crept into this crack. Twisting, rending their fattened sides 'til they bleed, snatching on to the sharp edges..." Makarov stopped typing and pushed the instrument aside so sharply that it crashed to the floor. Then he got dressed and went out.

Tattered gray clouds were tearing across the sky. Makarov calmed down a bit. His presentiment of imminent death had vanished somehow. "This is the world after my own heart," he thought, walking the filthy streets. "The foul rain, the scattered heaps of garbage, the scowling faces of the passersby..." On the other hand, it was possible that all this was a mere hallucination, and in fact the sun was shining, there were no garbage heaps at all and everyone passing by had joyful smiles on their faces. "Let's hope to God not," thought Makarov, plunging his hands into the pockets of his heavy overcoat. "I don't need that. I like it when it's — like this."

The beer joint was still closed, so Makarov decided to go to the movies. On account of the early hour he was the only one in the auditorium. He had to pay for five tickets (to cover the theater's expense for the show.). Makarov sat in the first row and lit a cigarette. The lights went down. The screen flickered with scenes of chases and firefights. But the alarm began to grow again in Makarov's mind. "What's going on?" he thought. "Time has stopped, and *they've* crawled in..." It seemed that, besides Makarov, no one had noticed...

What a joke. Time cracks, like an old statue, and everybody keeps on living like nothing's happened.

Makarov looked at his watch's glowing dial. Yes, time has stopped. But these others just keep on crawling in. They cut up their writhing, bleeding fingers... I wonder what their blood is like? Green? Or maybe black? Makarov undid the little strap on his wrist and, sticking the watch in his pocket, went out into the street.

He stepped out and — froze!

Instead of the filthy beer joint so dear to his heart, a trendy modern building with wide display windows was before his eyes. In one window a pretty girl was showing off her looks, in another pure-bred dogs happily bared their teeth...

The doors opened on their own, inviting Makarov to enter. And he entered.

III

Inside everything twinkled, gleamed and overflowed with iridescence.

The mirrored tiles on the floor. The mirrored counter of the bar. The brilliant white balls beneath the ceiling. The small stage crammed with tiny, multi-colored lights... Throughout the space stood small tables with pink table lamps... In other words, it was an elegant place.

It's just that... the door to the kitchen was slightly ajar, and behind it a bald dwarf with the stupidest grin was busying himself by a sink of dirty dishes; it's just that the bartender was... how do I put this... a hermaphrodite; it's just that the sad girl in the light-blue dress, sitting on the edge of the stage, looked painfully like a drowned corpse... Otherwise it was all just fine.

Makarov looked around. Dozens of mirrors gazed at him threateningly, with empty faces. He was not reflected in a single one.

"It's starting," thought Makarov.

The steward bustled across the hall, and rushed right over to him.

"Good evening, dear guest," he bared his teeth in an unpleasant grin.

Makarov looked at his hands. Both the steward's palms were covered in fresh cuts.

A huge saxophonist with an astonishingly ugly face appeared on the stage. One has only to look at his fish-like eyes. He started emitting hoarse, broken sounds from out of his sax. At this, the drowned girl climbed up onto the stage and began swaying in a slow dance.

The steward led Makarov to the farthest corner of the hall.

"Do you know the name of our little operation here?" the steward asked, partly turning away.

"I know," answered Makarov to himself. "The Trap."

"What'll we be having?" asked the steward officiously, seating Makarov behind one of the little tables.

"Blood," said Makarov.

"Excuse me?" replied the steward in confusion.

"You have blood on your chin," indicated Makarov, with a finger on his own chin.

"I cut myself," muttered the steward and, lightning-quick, lapped up the tiny red drop with his long tongue. "So what should I bring you?"

"Beer," said Makarov.

The steward walked off. The bald dwarf looked in from his dish-washing station in the kitchen. He scrutinized the entire hall. Catching sight of Makarov, the dwarf went over to him.

"Hey, Villy," he said in a squeaky voice. "How ya doin', buddy?"

"I'm not Villy," answered Makarov, frowning. The dwarf's high-pitched voice resonated unpleasantly in his ears.

"I read your latest book, Villy," continued the dwarf, sitting on a stool. "I thought it was crap."

The hall was filling up gradually. There were almost no free tables left. To the right of the dwarf sat a young woman with a pale face and bright lips that looked like smeared with blood.

"The typical vampire look," thought Makarov.

This was Fanny. (How did she wind up here? Who knows. Maybe she was just dreaming all this.

Fanny ordered a double Manhattan on the rocks and a crab salad.

"Hello," she said, looking at Makarov sidelong.

"You know me?" Makarov came to life.

"Of course," nodded Fanny. "We're stairwell neighbors."

"There's the writer's fame for you," gloomily reflected Makarov.

Musicians in gleaming gold jackets appeared on the stage. They all at once started banging on their instruments. The drowned girl began singing a song in English, in a low, hoarse voice.

The entrance door burst open with a crash. A cold wind rushed into the hall.

"Hey, somebody!" the girl yelled, interrupting her song. "Close the door, dammit, or the wind'll blow me away. Then I'll be — gone with the wind!"

Approving applause burst from various ends of the hall. But it seemed no one was getting up to shut the door.

Makarov stood and went up to the exit. Outside it was pouring rain. It was coming down so hard it looked pitch black out there. Makarov shut the door.

Again there sounded the sharp notes of the piano, the sax's wail, the guitar's weeping... The girl was more talking along with the music than singing.

Makarov returned to his seat.

"She's dead," said the waiter, setting down a mug of beer.

"Dead?" said a surprised Makarov.

"Yes. What're you so shocked at? You know how it's written in that book, 'The dead always outnumber the living.' "

"That's my book," said Makarov.

Fanny looked at Makarov. Oddly, the old writer's slovenly appearance aroused her.

"Have you ever wanted to die?" she asked.

"And you?"

"Why do you answer a question with a question?"

Makarov sipped his beer.

"Let's put it this way: I'm already dying. A writer who stops writing starts to die."

"So why don't you write?"

"Why?" Makarov hmmed. "Are you conscious of your own breathing?"

"Sometimes."

" 'Sometimes,' that's one thing. But if they were to pump all the air out of here and shove an oxygen cylinder in front of you with, say, five liters of air in it — then you'd probably start counting every gulp."

"You haven't answered my question."

Makarov knocked a cigarette out of the pack.

"The world's got too many questions that can't be answered," he said. "There is simply no answer."

After playing a few numbers, the musicians went over to the bar. The drowned girl sat down by Makarov. In fact, she'd stopped being a "girl" a long time ago. But never mind that.

"Thank you for closing the door," she said. "Otherwise I get this chronic cold." The girl stuck a cigarette into a white cigarette holder and started to smoke. "Do you like my singing?"

"Yes," Makarov admitted. "Very much."

"My voice is really kinda so-so, but it's good enough for this dump." She frowned through the cigarette smoke. "Won't you buy a girl a cocktail?"

Makarov ordered several cocktails.

When the waiter brought tall glasses with lemon slices wedged on top, the girl removed the slices and tossed them on the table. Then right away she polished off two glasses, one right after the other. Clearly, something wasn't going well in her life. Even if she was dead.

"Are you really dead?" asked Makarov.

"Mee-o-ow," meowed the girl in place of an answer. She was already pretty loaded.

"We'll see how dead you are in a minute," snickered the dwarf and, striking the little ignition wheel on his lighter, brought the tiny lick of flame right up to the girl's chin.

It smelled of burnt flesh.

"Ts-ts-ts," the girl playfully rattled her tongue.

"Well, this doesn't mean anything," muttered a disheartened Makarov.

IV

The musicians returned onstage and, in a relaxed manner, started playing "Where Wanes the Rosy World."

The corpse-girl touched the tips of her fingers to Makarov's unshaven cheek.

"You wanna go with me?" she asked.

"Later," answered Makarov.

"Later," she slowly repeated. "Don't you know there's no such thing as 'later'?"

"Ooh, you've cut to the very heart of the matter," said Fanny, smiling flaccidly.

Encouraged by this half-smile, the corpse-girl grabbed Fanny by the wrist.

"And you?" she whispered, panting. "Will you go with me?"

It seemed both girls were getting excited.

Fanny pulled back sharply, with a jerk, as if she'd been shocked by an electric current.

"Get away from me, kid," she spat out maliciously. "You stink all over — of earth."

The corpse-girl pulled her hand away.

"You shouldn't say that," she said, dovishly. "After all, you'll die someday too."

"I've died twice already," answered Fanny, irritably. "The first time when I was seven, on the operating table. The second time at seventeen, when I was hit by a car. So save it."

The dwarf slapped Makarov on the shoulder.

"Come on, now, Villy," he grinned. "It's like they're offering you a sunny day, the sea, a nude beach, and you say, 'No-o thanks, guys, I'd rather go to the basement where they axed a certain girl to death.'"

Makarov's insides all came apart. His nostrils caught the stomach-turning reek of blood. Trying to cover up the smell somehow, he finished off his beer at a gulp.

"What do you mean?" Makarov barely moved his lips.

"You know what," winked the dwarf.

The corpse-girl once again stroked Makarov's cheek.

"Would you like me to perform something just for you?" she suggested.

"Yes! Yes!" Makarov gratefully seized upon this proposal. "Please, sing 'The Oblivion Express.' Do you know that song?"

"No, I don't," answered the girl, with lustful fires again flaring in her brown eyes. "But for you I'll sing it."

The saxophonist picked up his sax. The guitarist turned up his amplifier. The pianist flopped down on the spinning stool. The corpse-girl took up the microphone and started singing in a hoarse voice, filled to the brim with a sweet bitterness:

> The Oblivion Express rushes through the night.
> A forgotten parrot in a forgotten cage
> Keeps shouting, "Br-r-azil."
> A forgotten cigarette smolders,
> A forgotten cup of tea sits on the table.
> And nearby, in the mirror
> The forgotten faces of people...
> Everything's forgotten that you can forget
> The Oblivion Express rushes on along a valley.
> Forgotten centuries pass,
> A forgotten river flows —
> Into a forgotten desert...
> There sounds a melody, forgotten long ago.
> Love sits forgotten on a shelf.
> Forgotten wolves follow the express.
> Forgotten, I gaze at them from a window.
> All this is so much like a forgotten movie.
> In it there also ran an express called "Oblivion"
> And a forgotten parrot in a forgotten cage
> Also cried, "Br-razil"...

There was a long saxophone solo... Across from Makarov, a little girl sat down, eating ice cream. Makarov shook his head. The vision disappeared.

"What's the matter, is your imagination playing tricks?" asked Fanny, knowingly.

"How'd she guess?" wondered a shocked Makarov to himself.

"I feel it," said Fanny. "I feel everything. Like a cat."

"I hate cats," spitefully squeaked the dwarf. "Revolting creatures."

Suddenly, from out of nowhere, a huge Great Dane appeared in the hall. Howling horribly, it charged Fanny. She seemed to be expecting this. A shot rang out. The dog fell to the floor, dead. Blood flowed from the bullet wound in its head.

The saxophonist stopped playing, jumped from the stage and ran over to the executed dog. Squatting, he carefully lay the dog's head on his lap.

"You!" the saxophonist spat out at Fanny. "You!"

"I'm so sorry," she said coldly, putting the gun away in her bag. "How much do I owe you?"

"I don't sell my friends," the saxophonist replied with a malign grin. "Especially the dead ones."

The bald dwarf grabbed hold of the dead dog by its hind paws and dragged it to the kitchen. A bloody trail stretched over the mirrored floor. The dancing resumed, as if nothing had happened.

The hall shook with the sound of music. The shining balls spun beneath the ceiling.

"They'll never forgive me for this," whispered Fanny.

Makarov heard her.

"Who'll never forgive you?" he asked.

Fanny didn't answer.

Beyond the kitchen door there formed a kind of "knot" or "clot" of danger. Makarov sensed it as a purulent boil, just about to burst open.

"I think we'd better get out of here," he said in alarm.

The bartender was approaching his table with a determined look.

"Look, man," he grabbed Makarov by the lapel of his jacket. "You gave me a counterfeit bill. Come on, let's go take care a' this."

"What're you talking about, a bill?! I haven't even been at the bar!" Makarov tried to tear himself away from the bartender's tenacious grip. But nothing doing.

Meanwhile, some big guys in leather jackets showed up in the hall.

There wasn't a second to lose.

Makarov jumped up, knocking his chair over, and gave the bartender a sharp kick in the groin. He got him right in the balls!

"Run!" he yelled to Fanny.

And they sprang out into the rain-filled night.

V

The night swallowed them up without a trace. They dissolved into a dense mixture of darkness and fog. And those who'd run out after them froze at the entrance, perplexed, fretfully gazing into the impenetrable wall of murk.

The cat-woman and the old writer ambled along the crooked little streets, seeing neither themselves nor each other. And only the tedious rain, settling on their faces as drizzle, reminded them obliquely of their continued existence on earth.

Fanny and Makarov walked in silence, as if they'd known each other a thousand years and had already talked through everything long, long ago.

"What are you thinking?" asked Makarov all the same, after tarrying a bit.

"Nothing," disclosed Fanny. "I don't think very often. I live by my instincts."

Once more they fell silent. A yellow moon showed through the tattered clouds. Next to it the distant stars glimmered. Things started swimming out of the receding fog: strange metallic constructions that resembled prehistoric animals; decrepit houses; rusted suburban train carriages with missing windows; next to the carriages, in a single heap, lay telephone booths — also rusted-out and windowless. An unseen bird cried out in the distance. And somewhere nearby a bell tolled; its resolute peal reverberated at length in the humid night air.

Without speaking they passed by a small shop selling women's underwear. In the display window lay a nude woman with a missing leg. She stared alluringly at Makarov. He quickened his pace telling himself it was only a mannequin.

The town seemed deserted. Even though it was actually not that late. On the contrary, it was early. "But it's daytime right now, isn't it?" Makarov realized. "Not night. So why's it so dark?"

Without meaning to, Makarov and Fanny were staring at each other.

"Don't I remind you of anybody?" asked Fanny with a smile.

"No," Makarov also smiled.

"I look like a cat."

"A cat?"

"Yeah. I even have little whiskers. You can't see them, but they're there. You want to touch them?"

Makarov ran his fingers along Fanny's lips, which were wet from the rain.

"You feel them?"

"Yes."

They walked out onto a lakeside and strolled along the shore, on a sandy beach littered with trash and dead fish.

The walk was starting to tire them out. And as soon as they realized this, they turned up right near their building. They went through the entrance hall and, climbing into the elevator cabin as narrow as a coffin. The dim light on the ceiling came on. The elevator cabin barely moved. Fanny stared fixedly at Makarov.

"You have light blue eyes," she said.

"So?"

"Most killers have eyes like that."

"I've never killed anyone, personally," Makarov answered, with a strained levity. "Honest."

Fanny didn't adopt his tone.

"We've all got skeletons in the closet," she asserted, adding: "Or a dead girl in the basement."

Makarov's heart started pounding madly. The elevator stopped.

They were home.

VI

Fanny rolled a portable bar into the room. Then, after disappearing into the kitchen, she brought in two large plates of roasted meat.

"Eat it with your hands," she said, setting the plates down on a low table.

"With my hands?" echoed Makarov. "You don't have any forks?"

"I do. But the sight of a man grabbing pieces of meat with his hands turns me on."

She switched on the radio. Music came on.

"Is this blues?" asked Fanny.

"It's entirely possible." Makarov knocked back a glass. The whiskey scorched his throat.

"And do you know what the blues is?"

The repetition of the same word was already making Makarov nervous. He knocked back another glass.

"No, I don't."

"The blues is when a good man feels bad."

"Words, words," thought Makarov, closing his eyes. "I'm so tired of words..." Fanny kept on saying something, though Makarov no longer took in the meaning of her remarks, but only their outer surface, somehow. They appeared before him in the shape of spiders, standing uneasily on slanted, shaggy legs.

Makarov opened his eyes. The spiders vanished. Fanny sat before him.

"I think," she said, "that a good book can only be written by a good person."

Makarov corrected her:

"It's not good people that write good books, it's good writers."

The telephone rang, piercingly. At the same time, outside there came the furious barking of dogs.

Makarov made a move to answer the phone.

"Don't!" Fanny cried straightaway. "Don't answer."

The phone rang and rang. Makarov restlessly tapped his fingers on the table. Fanny's anxiety had infected him.

At last, after a torturous pause, Fanny quietly said:

"I don't want to cause anybody ill fortune." And, after a short silence, she added: "Of course, I don't particularly want to cause them good fortune, either."

"What do you want?" Makarov stuck the end of a cigarette into the flame of his lighter.

"My desires are simple," she replied. "I want it to snow in winter, not rain."

"That's all?"

"That's all."

"You must be awfully disappointed, then. After all, it's been nothing but rain this winter."

Fanny shrugged.

"Not on your life. I'm actually quite pleased. Especially when you take into account that the dog I shot wasn't a dog at all."

"And who was it?" asked Makarov.

"Who," repeated Fanny with a bitter smile.

VII

Suddenly it was as if Makarov had a nervous breakdown. It happened to him often enough. It would come all of a sudden, out of nowhere — and carry him off to the boundless Cosmos. And leave his body behind. Just like now — it grabbed him and carried him off. He looked around. But there was no Earth! None!

"Hey, wake up," Fanny's voice brought Makarov back.

They were already in the bedroom, in bed. Fanny was completely naked. She lay on her back and rested her legs on Makarov's shoulders.

"Now I'm gonna cross my legs together," she said playfully, "and the great writer'll go bye-bye."

And then what had to happen happened.

"A-a..." moaned Fanny, her voice rising higher and higher.

"Look," said Makarov, barely containing his annoyance, "stop faking your orgasm."

Fanny settled down right away.

"I thought you'd like it," she said, and started smoking.

"I did like it," he replied, dryly. "Thank you."

"Don't mention it, pal." Fanny's mouth let out a smoke ring. "On the whole, though, men disgust me."

"Then why'd you sleep with me?"

"Solely out of respect for your literary talent," joked Fanny.

Makarov took her words at face value.

"Yes, well, there was a time when my novels enjoyed a colossal success," he said, assuming a dignified air. Then he wilted again almost immediately. "But, of course, everything good comes to an end sooner or later. Everything good in my life ended one not very fine morning, when I found my dead wife next to me in bed..."

Fanny said nothing. It was dark in the bedroom. Makarov saw only the little red ember of a cigarette and the green of Fanny's pupils.

"What about the little girl?" asked Fanny under her breath.

"What... little girl?" Makarov went cold.

"Your daughter... she's still there, isn't she... in the basement?"

Makarov's heart, tearing through his ribcage, broke out and stuck onto the wall with a succulent smack. Then it slo-o-wly slid down to the floor as a slimy, pathetic lump of flesh... Makarov saw all this so vividly it made him sick.

Fanny painfully plunged her sharp nails in his shoulder.

"You have to do it before midnight!" she hotly whispered. "Then the crack will close itself. And *they'll* die out... With no loophole."

"Do... what?" asked Makarov in a cracking voice.

"Pray. Get on your knees and whisper your prayers, and cross yourself. Then you'll see the flesh start to emerge, from out of the blood. And the child will stretch out its hands to you..." Fanny took a breath. "Just look and make sure that it's really *her*... Do you remember if she has any marks?"

"A ringlet!" Makarov remembered at once. "She should have a ringlet on her right little finger. A silver one."

"Quiet!" Fanny pressed a palm to his mouth. "You hear? *They're on their way!*"

VIII

Beneath a cold, starry night roamed a pack of dogs. They ran step for step with each other. Like wolves. Large, formidable beasts with bloodshot eyes, their snouts baring teeth. Up ahead ran the leader. A huge skewbald hound of uncertain breed. With its loathsome head to the ground, it greedily drew in the hated scent of Fanny the cat.

The pack burst headlong into a small courtyard. The leader powerfully launched itself from the asphalt with its legs, shooting upwards like an arrow. Ramming through the window glass with its snout, it crashed down on the floor of Fanny's apartment.

"Shoot!" she cried out hysterically. "Shoot!!"

Makarov fired. The screaming mass of pain writhed and twisted about the room, flattening everything in its path. Makarov fired again. The din was unbelievable. Someone was banging insistently at the door. Then they started pounding with their feet.

"What's going on in there?!" loud voices reached them from behind the door. "Open up right now!"

Makarov rushed to open.

"No! Don't!" Fanny caught hold of him. "*They're* over there too!"

Another gray creature flew in through the smashed window. Makarov, forgetting his pistol, kicked it in the snout... Now dogs were crawling out of the woodwork. Like cockroaches. The room filled with snarling, barking noises...

And suddenly... *at once — it all vanished.*

Silence reigned. Only the rumbling of the refrigerator reached him from the kitchen.

"Fanny," called out Makarov. "Fanny."

Silence. The wind moaned outside the window.

What's this?... Makarov trembled. The phone rang. Insistently. Aggressively. Makarov answered.

"Makarov?" asked a high-pitched voice.

"Speaking."

"Still kickin'?"

"Looks that way."

" 'Looks,' "... sniggered the voice. "An' maybe it ain't so?"

He heard short beeps, indicating the line had gone dead. Makarov didn't have enough mental wherewithal to replace the receiver. He simply unclasped his fingers and left it hanging on its cord.

"I have to go," thought Makarov.

He went into the hall, put on his overcoat. Then he opened the front door.

"Hey!" yelled Makarov. "Hey!"

No one answered.

He descended the stairs.

To the basement...

Once down there, he switched on a flashlight. The bright little circle of light danced along the dirty-gray walls, snatching from the darkness, in turn, some leaky pipes, soiled condoms, dead mice... It got hard to breathe all of a sudden. Like someone had forcibly pumped all the air out of the basement. (In point of fact, that was entirely possible.)

Makarov froze. He felt as if, instead of blood, boiling water raced through his veins. At that very second, from all directions, resounded cheerful music, you could hear boisterous D.J. voices — like several radio stations had come on at once. Makarov moved on. His flashlight suddenly went out. Makarov flicked the switch. To no avail.

"That's it," he said, like a man condemned.

"You just cross yourself," Makarov distinctly heard Fanny's voice. "Come on..."

Makarov made the sign of the cross over himself. This didn't make the room any brighter. But now he could see in the dark. "Like a cat," he thought. "Like Fanny."

The music and voices quieted down.

"My desires are simple," said Makarov out loud, "I'd like it to snow in winter..."

Thick snow fell from the ceiling.

"The blues," said Makarov, still louder, "is when a good man is feeling bad!"

A saxophone wailed gratingly. In the air hung the disfigured face of the saxophonist.

"How about a black girl with turned-out lips?" asked the visage, winking its fish-eye. "Huh?"

"What's this with a black girl you're pushing on me?" said an indignant Makarov. "I need the whole world, the Universe... and here you offer me some broad!"

The fish-eyed visage dissolved.

At last Makarov found what he was searching for. A small, dark puddle spread out over the irregularities in the floor. Makarov squatted down and plopped his palm down in the puddle. When he brought his hand back up to his face, he saw his fingers were covered in blood.

Makarov got on his knees and feverishly started praying, mixing up all the lines. The bloody puddle began, hurry-scurry, to shrivel, congeal... And now a child's little hand was already stretching itself out to him, with five tiny outspread fingers.

"Dasha," sighed a shaken Makarov.

Beep-beep-beep... whined the watch in his coat pocket.

Midnight had arrived.

There was no ringlet on the little finger.

IX

Makarov and Dasha stood on a platform. All around stirred a dense forest. Torn clouds concealed the sky. The little girl silently gazed down at her feet, indifferent to everything on earth.

"Dasha, dear" Makarov pronounced timidly, "the train's going to come in a minute, and we'll be going home."

The girl said nothing. "Fine," thought Makarov, "everything's alright." And he really did feel everything would be alright. But in fact everything was going all wrong. The sun disappeared, as if it had fallen into a void. The chill wind carried with it from somewhere the odor of mold.

"Dasha," said Makarov. "Dasha..."

The girl stubbornly kept silent. A freight train tore by. The caboose lights twinkled. Something was pouring down from the sky without let-up. Not quite rain, not quite snow... A railroad worker walked up to Makarov.

"A kitty," he pointed to the rails.

Makarov looked. On the rails lay the crushed carcass of a cat. In the very next instant Makarov saw that it was Fanny. He blinked in dismay. Fanny had once again turned into a cat.

"I want to be a cat," declared Dasha, suddenly, whimsically.

"A cat?" echoed Makarov.

"Yes."

"How about a mouse?" Makarov forced out a smile.

At that moment Dasha gave him a quick shove in the stomach with both hands. Makarov didn't even manage an "Ach!" before falling under the wheels of the next freight train. A smile lingered on his face, as if plastered there.

He remembered life as a *certain* autumn... as a chance glimpse in a window...

Eternal Return

Translated by José Alaniz

I

On the eve of the Assumption of the Holy Virgin, at the tail end of a hot August, a peasant named Yegor swayed onto a local train. He had been to the Sunday market in the town of Bezhetsk to sell his young bull Stepan. He'd gotten a good price and now, flush and tipsy, was on his way back to his native village of Pigsty, which certainly lived up to its name, resembling as it did the filthy sty of some derelict farmer.

Yegor reached the district center of Sonkovo, from where he had to take a bus, but just then (as so often happens with we Russians) he had a bright idea: Think I'll walk instead. It didn't occur to him that he had a good thirty versts to go and that it was getting dark.

Well, fools rush in where angels fear to tread, so twiddling his thumbs, son of a gun, off he went! He walked and walked — and soon the night caught up with him. He'd only tramped as far as Lbovo, about three versts from Sonkovo. Naturally he didn't want to spend the night outdoors: the mosquitoes would eat him alive, and he had all that money on him... He knocked at one house, then another... You know how Russians are — always responsive to someone in need. But somehow people's only response around here was to let their dogs loose. On and on Yegor went; nobody would take him in. He was completely desperate. He'd just have to lie down on the ground and cover himself with his hand.

Suddenly he saw, at the far end of the village (closer to the dense forest), a log hut. As old as old, the logs all black with age. No fence, grass knee-high, windows dark. Well, finders keepers —

it's abandoned. Yegor rushed there. He pushed the door open, went in, and was just able to make out the modest set-up: a table, bench, stove. Nothing dripping from above, no drafts from below. What's wrong with it? Without further ado, Yegor tossed his jacket on the bench and fell fast asleep.

He dreamed that he was in this same hut, but that all the things in it were from his own hut (the one in Pigsty). It wasn't yet night, but late evening. The lamp shone brightly, the brick stove was hot and the table set with the customary vodka, tomatoes, fried chicken, a chunk of fatback, this and that... By the stove, Yegor's wife Varya was fussing with an oven fork. Varya. Dead these ten years. She was all red in the face, making rolls.

Yegor raised himself up on one elbow, unable to believe his eyes: everything here was his own! Even the two pictures on the wall (he'd cut them out of a magazine). Actually, Yegor noticed, it wasn't all exactly like home. His icon — of the Holy Mother with baby Jesus on her left arm — wasn't hanging in its corner. And this wasn't just any icon; it was an antique. Yegor's mother had hung it up herself for protection. And it was gone. This very much disturbed and distressed Yegor. And a black cat kept darting about over the creaky floorboards! Yegor had never had a cat. Much less a black one. He looked hard at this one: the fur on its head was charred in places. This, too, came as an unpleasant surprise.

But Varya went right on poking with the oven fork, filling a bowl with ruddy rolls, sprinkling them with melted butter and sugar. Yegor loved rolls best in the world (after vodka, of course). But now they didn't tempt him — he couldn't bear even the sight of them. Yegor turned away, looked out the window and nearly swore: the stars in the dark sky were all topsy-turvy. The Great Bear was missing altogether. When the moon swam out from behind the clouds, Yegor became seriously alarmed. It wasn't the Moon at all, but some planet he'd never seen before — maybe twice the size. It wasn't yellow, but a sort of poisonous green. Varya had finished with the rolls, meanwhile, and was working at the table. She took a knife and started slicing the fatback. But today's a fast day, Yegor thought frantically, it's a sin to touch a knife. Varya went right on slicing, oblivious; when she'd finished she put the knife down and stared at Yegor. She looked at him intently, as if she'd never seen him before. The black cat jumped in on her lap and curled up in a ball. Prrrr, it purred, prrrr, not an affectionate purr, but a sinister one: prrrrr... as if it were growling. Varya stroked it and went on staring at Yegor.

Though he wasn't a coward, Yegor quailed, he was afraid.

Varya seemed to be talking to herself:

"Look at them beady little eyes, so shifty."

"What're are you talkin' about, Varya?" Yegor asked, his heart sinking to his boots.

"You know what," Varya replied with a mysterious smirk. "You know what... Tell us again, good friend, how you drove me to my death."

"Varya, how can you say that!" Yegor boiled over. "You know yourself you had double pneumonia. I got the doctor's certificate to prove it. The medical examiner's, too."

"Those certificates of yours," said Varya, scratching the charred patches on the cat's head, "are fakes." She looked ready to strangle him. Even the cat sensed something, and jumped out of her lap in fright.

Yegor felt suddenly cold inside, Death was so clearly in the air.

"What're you so scared for?" asked Varya, with that same mysterious smirk. "Don't worry. I won't touch you. I'll just say this, dear: I had a baby in my belly. Could already feel him kickin', but you sent us to the grave."

Varya gave a heavy sigh.

"What baby?" Yegor frowned with annoyance. "They opened you up! Weren't no baby in there. What do you think, the doctors don't know anything? Think they don't know a baby when they see one?"

"That's right," Varya insisted. "Didn't see mine. 'Sif you didn't know what our doctors're like."

Well, actually, that was true, Yegor agreed privately, recalling that at Shrovetide he had gone to have a bad tooth pulled, and lost two healthy ones instead. Another time, on Palm Sunday, a finger had a splinter and instead of taking it out, those bastards chopped the whole hand off. (True, it wasn't his hand, it was his neighbor Grisha's, but still they chopped it off.)

"Um hmm," Yegor drawled, lost in thought.

"Well, there you go," said Varya. "My baby's still tossin' about inside me."

"What d'you mean 'tossin'?" said Yegor in amazement. "When you been dead God knows how long!"

"I died, that's right," replied Varya. "But my baby's still tossin'."

"And... so?" Yegor couldn't see her point.

"So nothing," she said. "Gotta get it out." She paused, gave him a piercing look and added: "Specially since it's yours."

Yegor felt desperately afraid at first, but then his masculine pride took over.

"No you don't, no you don't!" he cried. "And as for whose baby it is, I wouldn't be so sure. I was away in the virgin lands then. In Kazakhstan."

Varya said nothing to that. But her face turned green, like the planet out the window. Two tiny tears rolled down her cheeks — both bloody. And from out of nowhere the black cat meowed: meeee-ooow-w-w-w-w-w....

Then Yegor woke up.

II

He woke up, and the sun was shining in the window. Our own earthly sun. Birds were singing in the trees; cocks were crowing back and forth. Thank goodness! Yegor jumped up, grabbed his jacket — and fled that accursed hut. It was early morning, the fields still swathed in mist, a high blue sky and not a single cloud; peasant women were herding cattle. Yegor ran along the hedges and the fences, but he couldn't stop wondering. Why did that strange hut make him dream such dreams? Think I'll ask someone.

Though Russian women are known for their beauty in distant lands, where they win all sorts of prizes, in Lbovo, for some reason, one woman was uglier than the next. Literally no one caught your eye. God forbid anyone should look like that. Still Yegor did find one more or less passable woman and put his questions to her.

"Hey there, whose hut is that?"

"Which'un?"

"That one over there, on the edge of the forest. All overgrown."

The peasant woman crossed herself and looked somber.

"Wicked place," she said. "A witch she lived there, but she ben dead five years. Ach, the harridan, ach, the ha-a-aridan. The things that harpy done! Why she deprived my'n husband Pyotr of his manly stren'th. Just lies abed now like a dullard. She ruined our neighbor's cow, too; 'steada milk Zorka started givin' blood. Lotsa blood, I swear, three buckets at a go. But bein' it ain't milk, can't drink much of it."

"Tell me," said Yegor, "did she have a black cat?"

" 'Course she did, a big one! Ach, plu-u-ug ugly devil. With charred patches here an' here." She pointed to her head. "They said it was a bungle, said she splashed it with a poisonous potion by accident."

Yegor's heart missed a beat. It all came back to him now: the cat did have charred patches, and exactly in the places where the woman had pointed.

The woman went on:

"And when she died, you won't believe it, but after the morgue she there lay dead in her hut for two whole weeks. Di'n't smell, di'n't rot. Just lay there in her coffin like she was alive. And they say that cat jumped into her coffin one night and curled up on 'er chest. Terrible! And when they buried her, the cat disappeared... Missy, Missy," she called tenderly to her cow. "Go on, darlin', nibble that grass."

Yegor shook his head at this curious story, and made for the bus stop. This was no place to be walking about. Soon, his own Pigsty appeared out the bus window, and his own dear house, and sweet Nyura, Yegor's second wife. Affectionate, talkative, hard-working. Yegor buried his face in her boundless bosoms, soft as feather pillows, and forgot all sorrows and misfortunes.

Then came the bitterly cold month of December, then Christmas drew nigh, Candlemass (when winter and summer meet) came and went... The nights became shorter, the days longer. Easter Sunday arrived in old Russia; then again the merry month of May, the Holy Trinity.

Another year passed; so life goes by, without us noticing.

Taken up by daily cares and chores, Yegor forgot about the strange dream he had, about his first wife Varya ordering him to pull the baby out of her belly. Summer came. And around the time of St. Peter's Fast, a man appeared asking for lodging and offering a tidy sum, too. He wore spectacles and looked a serious city fellow. He promised he'd be no trouble: he hadn't come for a rest, but to work in the country quiet. He had an odd name no one had ever heard before: Mr. Schulz.

Well, Yegor's house had a little room off to one side that no one used. It had a table, chair, trestle bed. And some extra money is never amiss. To make a long story short, they settled on the whole summer and soon Mr. Schulz moved into Yegor's little annex with his one small suitcase. He did as he said: for days at a time no one saw him or heard a peep out of him. He didn't even go down to the village stream. He sat in his room like a mouse in its hole. As agreed, Nyura left a pitcher of cow's milk by his door every morning, also sour cream and cottage cheese. Sometimes even this remained untouched. Yegor would go outside in the evening — and see the light burning in the annex. When he went out after midnight (to the outhouse), the light would still be on. And at dawn: the same thing. A couple of times he looked in on his lodger — wasn't dead, was he? No, he was alive, hunched over the table writing something.

Yegor had one sin: he was terribly curious. In fact, Mr. Schulz's mysterious behavior so troubled him, he was completely undone. He couldn't sleep and lost his appetite. Nyura started to grumble that Yegor was neglecting her at night, something he'd never been accused of before. Well, that did it! Enough! He couldn't stand it any longer! Yegor opened the door to the annex and strode in; Mr. Schulz didn't even look up, just went on writing.

"Excuse me kindly," Yegor said timidly. "Don't take me wrong. But what is it that you do in here from morning to night? If it's no secret, that is."

Mr. Schulz turned away from the table, took off his silver-rimmed spectacles and wiped them with a handkerchief. Without his spectacles he looked still more intelligent. And distinguished. Only a charred bit of skin by his hairline marred his appearance.

"Why no," he answered. "It's not a secret. It'll be my pleasure to tell you."

And he did.

III

This happened a long time ago, well before the Bolsheviks began ruling the roost. In this very part of the country there lived a Russian barin. His manor house, in fact, is now home to the collective farm pigsty. The barin's name was Pyotr Ilyich, just like Chaikovsky's. He was considered an educated man then — and not only then. He was clever. He was a friend of Pushkin's and something of an author himself; he wrote romantic stories in the manner of Marlinsky. Naturally, such a man could not bury himself away in the country. And he didn't. He spent the better part of every year traveling abroad, or living in Moscow and St. Petersburg. He had houses with servants everywhere. A very rich man, blessed with good health and looks to boot. But all Russians, as you know, have their eccentricities. They do not live by bread alone, they like a little spice and anguished soul-searching. Well, Pyotr Ilyich, too, had an eccentricity, or rather a weakness. He loved to flog into his young serf girls in the stable. He kept a little lash just for the purpose, leather, braided. This is why, despite a deep affection for their master, the peasants nicknamed him 'Savage'. Though, in all fairness, he never flogged a girl to death and always lavished gifts and money on them afterwards.

One day Pyotr Ilyich brought an actual Frenchwoman, straight from Paris, home with him to his estate. A delicate, ethereal creature, almost otherworldly. Her name was Louise Duval. She was a ballerina. She took to wearing a Russian peasant dress, braiding her hair, going barefoot, drinking kvass and eating cabbage soup. At dawn she would go down to the pond (now a mud puddle), perform a few fouettes and bathe. One day, unfortunately for her, she happened on Pyotr Ilyich in the throes of one of his fits. It was as if a demon had whispered in his ear: go on, go and give someone a good whipping. He seized his lash and dashed off to the garden, where he found Louise, fresh from her swim. Pyotr Ilyich grabbed her by her braids and dragged her off to the stable! There he flogged her. And flogged her — to death! (This was no Russian wench, after all. How much could a Frenchwoman take? Especially a ballerina?) Of course, there was also a misunderstanding. Louise could have screamed out. In French. She could have appealed, so to speak, to Pyotr Ilyich's essential goodness. But she had mistaken his crude treatment of her for frenzied passion. She apparently thought this Russian barin was just having a bit of fun. And even when she felt the first lashes on her soft shoulders, she attributed them to the ardor of the enigmatic Russian nature. And later... later it was too late. Pyotr Ilyich flew into a rage. She could have screamed in French, in Italian even — it wouldn't have helped.

When he came to his senses, Pyotr Ilyich's grief knew no bounds. He was so distraught that the locals feared for his sanity. Twice he ran down to the pond to drown himself; he seriously considered retiring to a monastery. Instead he went to St. Petersburg. There he found an old Chinaman, an embalmer, and brought him back to the estate. The Chinaman was a master of his art. Louise Duval lay in her coffin as if alive. In the cemetery, meanwhile, a small chapel had been built with stained-glass windows, a cupola topped with a ruby cross, and a statue of Louise in a marble coffin. The real coffin with the real Louise was in a small chamber beneath the chapel. Few knew that a tunnel had been dug from the manor house to this chamber. (Yegor nodded; yes, yes, he remembered the half-ruined chapel in the cemetery. Barefoot boys still played there. True, the stained-glass windows and ruby cross were long gone, but the statue with its nose broken off was still there.) No sooner had they buried the Frenchwoman than it was rumored that in the graveyard you could hear mysterious voices coming from underground. One holy wanderer swore to God that three hours past midnight he'd seen a woman in white, dancing among the crosses. In the next century, during the deadly thirties (again according to these same rumors), the Cheka started burying its victims in this cemetery. They even said that the last tsar and his family had been executed not in Yekaterinburg, but here. In short, said Mr. Schulz, it's a puzzling place in every respect."

Yegor had listened closely to this curious story.

"Well?" he asked.

"Well nothing," shrugged Mr. Schulz.

"But what is it you're busy with from morning to night?" Yegor persisted. "If it's not a secret, of course."

"Of course not," replied Mr. Schulz. "No secret at all. It'll be my pleasure to tell you."

And he did:

"I study infernology. Have you ever heard of such a science?"

Yegor shook his head — no, he hadn't.

"It's the science of Hell," explained Mr. Schulz. "Because according to my calculations, Hell is in Russia."

"How do you mean in Russia?" Yegor was stunned.

"Well, not exactly in Russia," Mr. Schulz corrected himself, "but under it. Right underneath us." He stamped the floor with the heel of his shoe.

"But... but... Why?" Yegor's breath was taken away.

"Where else could it be, if not under Russia?" said Mr. Schulz with conviction.

"Indeed," muttered Yegor, overwhelmed by such a weighty argument.

"By my theory," Mr. Schulz continued, lighting a cigarette, "Hell has three entrances and no exits. One entrance was in Atlantis and disappeared along with the island; where the second entrance is I don't know, though I suspect it may lie in..." Here Mr. Schulz looked round warily and, leaning closer to Yegor, whispered one word.

"That can't be!" exclaimed Yegor. "I don't believe it!!"

"But it's true!" said Mr. Schulz. "As for the third entrance..." He paused to exhale a blue-gray plume of smoke. "It's here."

"Where here?" Yegor looked around confused.

"In that graveyard where the Frenchwoman is buried."

There was a silence — broken only by the buzzing of a solitary fly about the room: bzzzzzzzzz-bzzzzzzzz-bzzzzzzzz...

IV

From that day on, relations between landlord and lodger were noticeably warmer. Before long Yegor and Mr. Schulz were the best of friends. Despite obvious differences in intellectual level. In the warm summer evenings they would sit out on the porch and talk and talk. About this and that. During one of those talks Yegor told Mr. Schulz about the dream he'd had the year before.

"Curious, curious," said Mr. Schulz, very interested. "You didn't happen to have that dream overnight on a Thursday, did you?"

"Yes, I did," Yegor recalled, "it was late Thursday night or early Friday morning."

"Then it's prophetic," declared Mr. Schulz. He became so abstracted that Yegor had made up his mind to go to bed when his lodger suddenly roused himself and said, pointing to the sky:

"Look, Yegor, there's no moon."

"What of it?" Yegor didn't understand. "The wind'll drive the clouds away in a minute, and it'll come out."

"No, it won't. Today is the nineteenth lunar day — a Satanic day when the forces of darkness revel."

"What does that mean?" asked Yegor.

"It means," said Mr. Schulz, "that the entrance to Hell is open."

He looked expectantly at Yegor who began to fidget.

"And you... want to..."

"Why not?"

"But we won't be able to see anything," Yegor tried to dodge.

"I have a flashlight. Battery-powered."

"But... but..." Yegor couldn't think of what to say to that. All he wanted was to curl up next to Nyura's warm flank, but now instead it looked as if he were headed somewhere a lot warmer — and lower down. "But wait," he finally found the words, "what if they come at us?"

"We'll defend ourselves," said Mr. Schulz unperturbed. "I have a pistol, a long-barreled Colt .45. For just such an occasion."

"Umm... I don't know," Yegor scratched his head. "Maybe I should tell Nyura."

"Don't."

"Why?"

"What do you think she'll say? 'Go, Yegor dear, go to Hell'?!"

"You're right," he agreed.

Mr. Schulz leapt up from the porch.

"I'll go and fetch my carpetbag, you take an axe and two shovels."

"What do we need shovels for?" said Yegor surprised.

"While we're at it, we'll exhume your wife," Mr. Schulz explained brightly. "Wouldn't you like to see what's left of her?"

"Well, I guess so," Yegor mumbled, uncertain.

That graveyard could give anyone the willies in the daytime, let alone on a moonless night. In the driving rain. Walking through the village, everything seemed all right. Dogs barked in the yards, lights glimmered in the windows. But as soon as the village was behind them and the dark pitch-black, Yegor lost heart. He shambled along after the energetic Mr. Schulz, dragging his heels... Then an eagle owl started hooting, the pest! (Yegor's stomach was all in knots because of that hooting.) They felt the cool of the little river — it meant they were almost there.

As soon as they arrived, the rain stopped. And the wind quieted. Not a single branch stirred.

It was quiet. Eerily quiet.

They found Varya's grave and set to work. In less than an hour their spades banged against the lid of the coffin. They hauled it up out of the grave: a good oak coffin, none the worse for wear; only the cloth covering had rotted. Yegor pried open the lid with his axe — it came right off. And before them lay the dead Varya. Yegor stared wide-eyed at his former wife. After ten years of lying in the earth, she seemed not to have changed at all. If anything, she'd gotten prettier.

Mr. Schulz shone his light right in her face.

"Well, well, well," he whistled. "If it isn't Louise Duval."

"What Louise Duval?" Yegor didn't remember at first.

"Why, that Frenchwoman, whom Pyotr Ilyich flogged to death. Remember, I told you all about her."

"You're mistaken, Mr. Schulz," Yegor began to fret. "This is my first wife. Varya."

Mr. Schulz, as usual, became abstracted, then said:

"I've got it. Your wife was a phantom. In actual fact she died in the last century. Congratulations, Yegor, you lived with a phantom. But how is it she's so well preserved, I wonder. Here, you hold the flashlight," said Mr. Schulz and quickly reached into his carpetbag.

Only now did Yegor notice that Varya's belly was distended,

as if she were pregnant. Mr. Schulz produced a scalpel, thrust it into Varya's abdomen, and made an incision through the shroud.

And then... and then.... Yegor didn't realize at first what had happened. Suddenly there was a piercing squeal and a terrible stench; then something slimy, bloody and shaggy burst from Varya's belly (to the frightened Yegor, it looked like a monkey) and rushed off!

"Catch it! Catch it!" cried Mr. Schulz.

But there was no catching that thing! The little monster, swift as a racehorse, galloped off among the graves. They only just managed to catch a glimpse of it.

Mr. Schulz was in a state of wild excitement.

"I knew it!" he rubbed his hands together with glee. "I knew it! What a splendid practical affirmation of my theoretical computations! Hang on to your hats, gentlemen anthropologists! I may win the Nobel!"

Yegor maintained a bewildered silence.

"Who do you suppose that was?" Mr. Schulz looked merrily at his friend.

"Well... I'm not sure... My little boy, probably."

"Ha! Little boy? Little boy, my foot! That was a skunk, I tell you! An actual skunk!"

"What? A what?"

"A little animal," Mr. Schulz explained more calmly. "It lives in North America and in appearance resembles our local polecat. But that's not the point. I chose that approximate name simply to designate the phenomenon. Who this one is, I don't know. I suspect it may be of supernatural origin." Mister Schulz lit a cigarette and went on: "Strange tiny creatures make their way into the bodies of dead women through the vagina and grow to adulthood there. For them a woman's womb is the best nutrient medium. Outwardly, the woman appears to be pregnant — only it lasts much longer than nine months. Once it has matured, the skunk gnaws its way out of the dead woman's abdomen. They have adapted so well to human society that it's practically impossible to catch sight of them. Furthermore, all skunks are small and venomous..."

Yegor stiffened. A suspicious sound seemed to be coming from Varya's grave. He shone the flashlight in that direction and...

Couldn't believe his eyes.

"Mr. Schulz," he wheezed. "L-look..."

But Mr. Schulz was already looking.

"A-a-a-ah," he drawled.

For Varya's grave had become a yawning hole. And through this hole, far below, you could see land. They felt as if they were gazing down from a great height. From an airplane. (Yegor had taken a plane once to visit his mother-in-law in Taganrog.) And all along this mysterious surface, as far as the eye could see, bonfires burned. Bonfires, bonfires...millions of them! Clods of black smoke billowed up to the sky (to where Yegor and Mr. Schulz were standing). Through the smoke human wails rose up, shrieks and screams. It was as if one continuous moan were coming out of the grave. A moan filled with such suffering... such suffering... Yegor stood there with Mr. Schulz, unable to move. Dumbfounded. Just then, from behind the nearest cross, the skunk appeared. Already clad in rags and tarpaulin boots, it stole up behind Mr. Schulz and shoved him into the grave. And Yegor after him.

V

Yegor came to underground. Dim bulbs dotted the walls, somewhere in the distance water was dripping: drip-drip, drip-drip... the sound resounded so. Mr. Schulz was sitting beside him. Alive and unharmed.

"Mr. Schulz," said Yegor, " where are we? In Hell?!"

"I don't believe so," said Mr. Schulz, after some thought. "See, the rails there."

Yegor looked down: indeed, there were rails.

"Maybe this is the metro?"

"The tunnel is too narrow for the metro," said Mr. Schulz. "The cars wouldn't fit."

"But how'd we get here?" Yegor scratched his head.

"The devil knows," said Mr. Schulz, scratching the charred patch on his head. "But I think we should get out of here as quickly as possible."

He stood up and walked quickly along the tunnel. Yegor trotted after him.

"But whatta you think happened to us?" Yegor went on wondering aloud. "Hmm, Mr. Schulz?"

"I have no idea."

"But was that Hell we saw?"

"I doubt it," Mr. Schulz shook his head. "I believe that was an ordinary hallucination caused by the psychic energy emanating from your dead wife. Or rather from the phantom. I've heard of such things."

"But then..." Yegor stopped short.

The rails suddenly ended, the tunnel expanded and they found themselves in an enormous vaulted space, whose floor was piled high with dead bodies.

"Back, quick!" yelled Mr. Schulz. He led the way at a run, taking two sleepers at a time. Yegor followed suit.

"This is that place I was telling you about," Mr. Schulz explained, panting. "Remember? Where the Cheka dumped the bodies of the ones they'd shot..."

Suddenly, from around a bend, some people appeared.

"Hold it right there!" they yelled. "Or we'll blow your brains out."

They fired a couple of warning shots: bang! bang! bang! The bullets whizzed by Yegor's ear: fyut! fyut! fyut!

Yegor and Mr. Schulz froze in their tracks. What else could they do? The strangers searched them, confiscated Mr. Schulz's Colt .45 and led them away with their hands bound and eyes blindfolded.

They walked uphill, then downhill, then were driven somewhere on something (most likely a hand cart). When they arrived, they went up some steep stairs, heard a lot of cursing and banging of doors, smelled cheap tobacco. At last the blindfolds were removed (their hands remained tied). They found themselves in a large room with a table. Sitting on the table was a scowling dwarf with a face like a lump of boiled beef and a cigarette of sorts dangling from his mouth.

"That's our skunk," Mr. Schulz whispered to Yegor.

Yegor stared: it was him.

Just then the door opened to reveal a strapping fellow wearing a tall Caucasian fur hat and carrying a rifle.

"Comrade Drachenko," he reported, "we've brought the kulaks from the district center. Where do we put 'em? The cellars are full up."

"Full of what?" asked the skunk.

"Nuns."

"Put 'em up against the wall!"

"Put who up against the wall?"

"The nuns."

"And the kulaks in the cellars?"

"No," said the skunk. "Put them up against the wall, too."

"But then who do we put in the cellars?" the big fellow was still confused.

"Nobody. Everyone up against the wall! And the requisitioned potatoes in the cellars."

"And these two up against the wall, too?" he pointed his rifle at Yegor and Mr. Schulz.

"These two?" the skunk seemed suprised. "Lemme get a look at 'em."

He looked at them. Intently. First at Yegor, then at Mr. Schulz.

"Yeah," he nodded, "liquidate them too."

Yegor and Mr. Schulz were led along a short corridor to a small interior courtyard, put up against a brick wall. And shot.

VI

Once again Yegor came to. This time inside a glass coffin. "Have the Chekists gone and given me a Christian burial?" Yegor wondered as he looked around. He was in a small room, hung with carpets. There was even a carpet on the ceiling. Yegor climbed out of the coffin and saw... Varya. Alive. Standing there with her hair down, in a long diaphanous gown. Yegor gasped. Varya gasped. Yegor felt his face. Varya felt her face. Yegor tensed. Varya tensed. Yegor stamped his foot! So did Varya! Then it dawned on Yegor: he was Varya! And he was standing in front of an ordinary mirror. Yegor paced the floor, back and forth. What a strange feeling: his chest was pushing him forward, his behind was pulling him back. How bizarre!

He heard a cautious knock at the door. Then a voice — a very familiar one.

"Mademoiselle Duval," it purred, "may I come in? It's me, Pyotr Ilyich."

"Of course," said Yegor, shocked at the feminine sound of his own voice.

The door opened and in strode Mr. Schulz in an old-fashioned suit. Or maybe it was his phantom (Yegor was thoroughly confused by now). He walked up to Yegor, or rather to Varya, or actually to Mademoiselle Duval, and kissed her hand.

"How did you sleep, my dear Louise?" he asked.

"Pretty well," said Yegor. "All right."

Pyotr Ilyich held on to Yegor's hand, stroking the girlish fingers.

"I've come for you," he purred. "Do me the honor of dining with me by candlelight." Suddenly he grabbed Yegor in a vice-like embrace.

"What! What! What!" wailed Yegor, flabbergasted.

"Mademoiselle Duval... Louise... Louisatchka..." Pyotr Ilyich murmured feverishly, covering Yegor's face with passionate kisses. "Please... I beg you... one night..."

Before Yegor knew where he was, Pyotr Ilyich had swept him up in his arms and carried him to the door. Then down a winding corridor, at the end of which he pressed a button in the wall. The wall slid open to reveal a bedroom.

Pyotr Ilyich poured some wine from a crystal decanter into crystal glasses.

"Have some of this, Louisatchka," he handed a glass to Yegor. "It's your favorite. Burgundy."

Yegor tasted it. To tell the truth, it wasn't that good. On the weak side. Top-shelf stuff is much better.

Pyotr Ilyich was already pulling Yegor toward the bed, gently but firmly.

"Lousatchka," he whispered hoarsely, "you promised we would today. On the anniversary of your death."

Yegor now realized that if he were to remain incognito, he

would have to let Pyotr Ilyich... The mere thought burned him up. That's all I need, might even end up havin' to give birth!

"But you promised, Louise," Pyotr Ilyich was on fire. "You promised..."

"I didn't promise you anything, Mr. Schulz," said Yegor coldly. "You're making it up."

Pyotr Ilyich jerked back, as if someone had walloped him on the forehead.

"Yegor?!" he exclaimed. "Is that you?"

"Me," said Yegor.

Mr. Schulz burst out laughing. He laughed and laughed... He collapsed on the bed he laughed so hard, tears streaming down his face.

"I can't stand it!" he writhed, practically in convulsions.

"You think it's funny..." Yegor sighed heavily. "But what about me? Can't even do my business the normal way."

Mr. Schulz finally stopped laughing and lit a cigar.

"Don't worry, Yegor," he said, puffing away. "You know what Eastern wisdom says: 'Woman, do not grieve that you are a woman, for in the next life you shall be a man. Man, do not celebrate your manhood, for in the next life you shall be a woman.' "

"I don't understand, Mr. Schulz," Yegor shrugged his soft shoulders.

"Then I'll explain." And he explained: "Many people, especially those born under the sign of Cancer, remember their past lives. But you, Yegor, strange as it may sound, remember your future. To put it more simply, the French ballerina Louise Duval will, in her next life, become the Russian tractor driver Yegor Ryabchikov. Now do you understand, Louisatchka?" Mr. Schulz winked.

Yegor understood nothing.

"But what about you?" he asked. "You were a man, an' still are."

"It's completely different in my case," replied Mr. Schulz. "I, if you must know, am not really human."

"Well, then, what are you?" Yegor wondered. "A skunk?!"

"No, not a skunk, either." Mr. Schulz was silent for a while, then added meaningfully: "Do you remember the black cat with charred patches on its fur?"

Yegor looked up:

"Well?"

"I keep going round in circles with you. Figure it out for yourself..." Mr. Schulz tapped his forehead with his index finger, "you ass!"

Yegor sniffed.

"Something's burnin'," he said. "And sounds like someone's yellin'."

Mr. Schulz sniffed the air and listened.

The thin curtains over the windows glowed red. Mr. Schulz jerked them open. Outside everything was on fire! The house, the wings, the stable, even the forest in the distance. In the courtyard, shadows rushed to and from in the inferno's glow.

"What the devil?!" said Mr. Schulz, bewildered.

"Now I get to explain," said Yegor, feeling an odd satisfaction. "The peasants decided to torch you! Well, hang on! They'll be here any minute with pitchforks!"

And indeed. The doors burst open and bearded peasants with pitchforks, axes and wild eyes surged into the bedroom.

"Aha-a!" they howled, "So yer the infernal wizard with the witch for a lovress!"

"Gentlemen! Gentlemen!" the terrified Mr. Schulz babbled, his voice breaking.

The "gentlemen" jabbed their pitchforks in his face and forced him up against a wall covered over with Chinese silk. Before Yegor could get a word out, they took an axe to his exquisite French head and split it open like a ripe melon.

VII

This time Yegor came to in a public toilet. By the urinals.

A young policeman was prodding him with the heel of his boot.

"Come on, you drunk, get out of here," he was saying, squeamishly.

Yegor got up from the grimy, slimy floor and wandered off. He looked like a tramp. Everything on him was ripped and filthy. His head was pounding, as if someone had been banging it against something (someone had). He went out into the street and damned · if he wasn't in the train station in Bezhetsk where he'd been a year ago when he brought his young bull Stepan to market. And there was the local train to Sonkovo. Yegor got on it. Of course, he hadn't bought a ticket — how could he? Anyway. The train pulled out.

A woman with all sorts of bundles and bags sat down opposite Yegor. Strapping, big-bosomed, she reminded him a bit of his Nyura. Yegor lowered his eyes. Looking like a tramp made him feel self-conscious.

Suddenly he noticed a ticket lying on the floor. Yegor edged it toward him with one foot, bent over and picked it up. Just in time, too.

"Tickets, they're checking tickets," the warning spread through the car. Conversations broke off; newspapers stopped rustling; little children stopped screaming. They were all waiting for something. "What?" wondered Yegor. On top of that, the train came to a stop. In the middle of an empty field. The car door slid open, and two ticket collectors appeared. Young men in black uniforms, with short-barreled submachine guns.

"Have your travel documents ready, please," said one politely.

They proceeded down the aisle. You could have heard a pin drop.

"Your ticket," the collector addressed Yegor.

Yegor produced the found ticket. The collector turned to the bosomy woman.

"Your ticket, miss."

The woman dug in one pocket of her faded cardigan, then in another. Her face became pitifully distorted; her eyes began darting about.

"I bought one, I did..." she looked up pleadingly at the boy-collector.

"Don't you worry," he tried to calm her. "Look in your bag. I'll wait."

The woman went feverishly through all her bags and bundles. Nothing.

"But I bought one!" she sounded hysterical. "I swear I did!"

"What are you so nervous about?" the collector smiled. "Let me help you." And, gathering up her things, he walked down the aisle.

The woman trudged after him looking perplexed.

"I bought one... I bought one..." she kept saying tearfully.

"What the devil?" Yegor didn't understand. "Maybe I should give that woman her ticket back? She's so broken up about it..." Besides the bosomy woman, the ticket collectors caught three other people without tickets: two little girls (twins) and an old man with a gray beard. They were taken off the train, lined up in the field and shot. A whistle blew and the train was off again. The wheels banged and rumbled happily. The tension in the car eased. People started talking, newspapers began rustling. Only Yegor was in a cold sweat and muttering gloomily to himself, "Can't believe it... Can't believe... Can't believe it..."

As soon as he got to Sonkovo he begged enough money to buy a bus ticket to his village of Pigsty. Out the dirt-smeared windows, Yegor saw dear, familiar landmarks. He calmed down. He was nearly home and already imagining how he'd bury his face in Nyura's soft bosom...

He opened the door, walked in and what did he see on the bench but a hideous old hag with a black cat on her lap. The same black cat. The hag raised her wrinkled face to Yegor and she started howling through toothless gums:

"Satan! Satan! Satan! Out of my sight! Out of my sight! Out of my sight!"

Yegor felt as if he'd been scalded with boiling water. This was his very own Nyura!

The rest Yegor couldn't remember too well. It was like being hangover. Some people ran into the hut, bound his hands and threw him into the cellar. Later a police van with a little barred window pulled up. Two dwarf policemen drove Yegor to Sonkovo. To prison.

They charged him with three offenses right off the bat. The first offense: cannibalism. Forty years before Yegor had supposedly killed and eaten citizen Pyotr Ilyich Schulz. The second offense: treason against the Motherland. While working in the virgin lands of Kazakhstan, Yegor had evidently been recruited by Kazakh intelligence. The third offense: theft. Yegor's little bull Stepan was apparently stolen property.

The trial took place on the eve of the Feast of the Tikhvin Virgin. In the courtroom, they put Yegor inside a cage, like a dangerous criminal, with armed soldiers on either side.

"All stand! The court is now in session!" cried the secretary, a young woman.

Presiding at the trial was Sofron Spiridonovich Selivyorstov — another dwarf, but with a pimply face and flanked by two lickspittles for jurors.

No sooner had the court come into session, than the judge withdrew to confer. Soon after Sofron Spiridonovich triumphantly read out the verdict.

Yegor was sentenced to death by splitting.

What this was exactly, his talkative lawyer explained to him after the trial.

"Splitting, Yegor Timofeich, was the most popular form of capital punishment in old Russia, and today it's enjoying a revival. Unlike electrocution, splitting requires no special equipment. The criminal's feet are tied to two young trees that have been pulled down to the ground with ropes. Then the trees are let go. And the criminal's soul flies up to heaven..." Seeing the change in Yegor's face, the lawyer hastened to add: "Don't worry, Yegor Timofeich. In your name, I've already appealed to the Supreme Court. The splitting may be commuted to drawing and quartering. Don't lose hope."

"Thanks," babbled poor Yegor. "I won't."

In early autumn, right after the Feast of St. Michael, the doors of the death chamber opened and Yegor was led out to the prison yard, where two beautiful white birches grew. They'd been specially planted, just the right distance apart. Guards pulled the birches down to the ground and tied Yegor's feet to them. Then they let the trees go, to the applause of assorted onlookers... And Yegor's soul flew up to heaven.

Afterwards it was reported that while in prison Yegor had prayed quite zealously. He'd been asking God to send down his

Heavenly Angels to save him. But not every prayer makes it all the way to our Lord.

They also said that while Yegor's remains were being interred a black cat with charred patches of fur on its head had appeared from out of nowhere. And jumped into the hole. They tried to coax it out but it wouldn't come. So they buried the live cat with the dead Yegor.